A BRIDGE TO THE STARS

A BRIDGE TO THE STARS

Henning Mankell

Translated by Laurie Thompson

First published in Great Britain in
2005 by Andersen Press Limited
This Large Print edition published
by AudioGO Ltd
by arrangement with
Andersen Press Limited 2011

ISBN: 978 1405 664059

Text copyright © Henning Mankell,
1990
Original title: *Hunden som sprang
mot en stjärna*
First published in Swedish by Rabén
& Sjögren Bokförlag
English translation ©
2005 Laurie Thompson

Printed and bound in Great Britain by
CPI Antony Rowe, Chippenham and Eastbourne

1

The dog.

That was what started it all.

If he hadn't seen that solitary dog, nothing might have happened. Nothing of what later became so important that it changed everything. Nothing of what was so exciting at first, but became so horrible.

It all started with the dog. The solitary dog he'd seen that night last winter when he'd suddenly woken up, got out of bed, tiptoed out to the window seat in the hall and sat down.

He had no idea why he'd woken up in the middle of the night.

Maybe he'd had a dream?

A nightmare that he couldn't recall when he woke up. Or maybe his dad had been snoring in the bedroom next to his own? His dad didn't often snore, but sometimes there might be an occasional one, a bit like a roar, and then it would be all quiet again.

Like a lion roaring in the winter's night.

But it was when he was sitting by the window in the hall that he saw the solitary dog.

The window had been covered in ice crystals, and he'd breathed onto the glass so that he could see out. The thermometer showed nearly thirty degrees below zero. And it was then, as he sat looking out of the window, that he'd caught sight of the dog. It ran out into the road, all on its own.

It stopped underneath the streetlamp, looked and sniffed in all directions, and set off running again. Then it vanished.

It was a familiar kind of dog, common in northern Sweden. A Norwegian elkhound. He'd managed to see that much. But why was it running around just there, all alone in the wintry night and the cold? Where was it heading for? And why? And why did it look and sniff in all directions?

He'd had the impression that the dog was frightened of something.

He'd started to feel cold, but he stayed in the window, waiting for the dog to come back. But nothing happened.

There was nothing out there, only the cold, empty winter's night. And stars glittering in the far distance.

He couldn't get that solitary dog out of his mind.

Lots of times that winter he'd woken up without knowing why. Every time, he got out of bed, tiptoed over the cold cork tiles and sat down on the window seat, waiting for the dog to come back.

Once he fell asleep on the window seat. He was still there at five in the morning when his dad got up to make coffee.

'What are you doing here?' his father asked after shaking him and waking him up.

His father was called Samuel, and he was a lumberjack. Early every morning he would go out into the forest to work. He chopped trees down for a big timber company with an unusual name. Marma Long Tubes.

He didn't know what to say when his

3

dad found him asleep on the window seat. He couldn't very well say he'd been waiting for a dog. Dad might think he was telling lies, and Dad didn't like people who didn't tell the truth.

'I don't know,' he said. 'Maybe I was sleepwalking again?'

That was something he could claim. It wasn't absolutely true, but it wasn't a lie either.

He used to sleepwalk when he was little. Not that he remembered anything about it. It was something his dad had told him about. How he'd come walking out of his bedroom in his nightshirt, into the room where his father was listening to the radio or studying some of his old sea charts. Dad had taken him back to bed, but in the morning he couldn't explain why he'd been wandering around in his sleep.

That was ages ago. Five years ago. Nearly half of his life. He was eleven now.

'Go back to bed,' said his dad. 'You mustn't sit here and catch your death of cold.'

He snuggled back into bed and listened to his dad making coffee, preparing the sandwiches he would take into the forest with him, and eventually he heard the front door closing.

Then everything was quiet.

He checked the alarm clock by his bed, on a stool he'd been given as a present for his seventh birthday.

He hated that stool. It was his birthday present, but he'd really wanted a kite.

He felt angry every time he saw it.

How could anybody give a stool to somebody who wanted a kite?

He could sleep for two more hours before he'd have to get up and go to school. He pulled the blanket up to his chin, curled up and closed his eyes, and the first thing he saw was that dog running towards him. It was running silently through the winter's night, and perhaps it was on its way to a distant star?

But now he was sure that he was going to catch that dog. He would entice it into his dream. They could be friends there, and it wouldn't be as cold as it was outside in the wintry night.

He soon fell asleep, the lumberjack's son, whose name was Joel Gustafson.

It was in the winter of 1956 that he saw that solitary dog for the first time.

And that was the winter when it all happened.

All that stuff that started with the dog . . .

2

The house where Joel lived with his father, Samuel, was by the river.

The spring floods would come surging and thundering down from the distant mountains beyond the dark forests. The house was where the river curved round before continuing on its long journey to the sea.

But now it was winter, and the river was asleep under its white blanket of snow and ice. Ski tracks scratched

6

stripes into the white snow.

Down by the river Joel had a secret.

Close by the stone buttresses supporting the big iron bridge where trains shuddered past several times a day was a big rock that had split into two.

Once upon a time the rock had been completely round. The crack had divided it into two halves, and Joel used to pretend that it was the earth. Whenever he crawled into the crack, where it smelt of damp moss, he would imagine being deep down inside the earth that he actually lived on.

A secret was being able to see what other people didn't see.

When he lay inside the crack, he used to think that he could change reality into whatever he liked.

Dancing around in the furious eddies and whirlpools caused by the spring floods were not logs, but dolphins.

The old uprooted tree that had stuck fast on the sandbank where Mr Under, the horse dealer, used to moor his rowing boat was a hippopotamus sticking its enormous head out of the water. And there were crocodiles under the surface of the water. Lying there, waiting to pounce on their prey.

Inside the crack in the rock Joel used to embark on his long journeys. In fact Joel had never been beyond the dark forests. He had never seen the sea. But that didn't matter. He would go there one of these days. When his dad had finally decided to stop working as a lumberjack. Then they'd go off travelling together.

In the meantime he could lie in the crack in the rock and go off on journeys of his own. He could imagine that the river was the strait between Mauritius and Réunion, the two islands off Madagascar. He knew what it was like there. His dad had explained how careful you had to be when sailing through that channel. There were dangerous sandbanks hidden just beneath the surface, and if your ship capsized it would sink four thousand metres to the bottom.

Joel's dad used to be a sailor. He knew what he was talking about.

When Joel saw dolphins and hippos in the river, it was his father's stories coming to life in his mind's eye. Sometimes he would take one or two of his father's sea charts down to the rock with him, to make it easier to transform the river into the other world.

Now that Joel was eleven years old, he knew that it was all make-believe. But it was important to take it seriously. If he didn't, he'd be betraying his own secret world.

In winter the enormous lump of rock would be covered in snow. He didn't go there so often then. Just occasionally he'd ski down the slope to the river, to make sure that the rock was still there. He'd establish a ski track round the rock, and think that it looked a bit like a fence. Nobody would be able to cross it and take possession of his rock.

It was in winter when they used to sit in the kitchen, Joel and his dad, and Joel would listen to all the stories.

In a glass case over the stove was a model ship. She was called *Celestine*, and his father had bought her from a poor Indian hawker in Mombasa. When his dad hung up his wet woollen socks to dry underneath her, the glass would mist over and Joel would imagine *Celestine* adrift in a thick cloud of fog, waiting for a wind to blow up.

He used to think something similar about the house they lived in. That it wasn't really a house but a ship that was riding at anchor by the river, waiting for a favourable wind. A wind that would blow them down to the sea. The rickety fence was in fact a ship's rail, and the attic flat they lived in was really the captain's cabin. The rusty old plough half buried in the abandoned potato patch was the ship's anchor.

One of these days the house they lived in would be set free. The anchor would be hauled aboard and then they would start gliding down the river, past the headland with the old dance pavilion. Just past the church they would be swallowed up by the endless forest . . .

'Tell me about the sea,' Joel used to beg.

Dad would switch on the radio and twiddle a knob until there was nothing to be heard but a murmuring sound.

'That's what the sea sounds like,' he would say. 'Close your eyes and imagine it. The sea that goes on and on for ever.'

They used to cuddle up on the kitchen bench when his dad felt like talking about all the remarkable things he'd experienced as a sailor. But sometimes he didn't feel like talking about it. Joel never knew when that would happen. Sometimes his dad came home from work with his nose frozen stiff and his socks wet through. But he was humming a tune and stamping his feet and snorting like a horse feeling pleased with itself as he shook off all the snow in the entrance hall, then sat down at the table and asked Joel to help him pull his boots off.

Joel would have boiled some potatoes when he got back from school, and if his dad was in the right mood he might well start talking about his adventures, once they'd finished eating and doing the washing up.

But sometimes there would be the sound of heavy steps on the stairs, a deep sigh as he pulled off his thick jacket; his face would be grim, his eyes averted.

Then Joel knew that he needed to be careful. Mustn't make a noise, mustn't ask about anything that he didn't need to know. Just set the table, serve up the potatoes, eat in silence the food his father prepared in the frying pan, then withdraw to his room at the earliest opportunity.

Two things were hard to cope with.

Not knowing why, and not being able to do anything about it.

Joel suspected that it must have something to do with his mother, and with the sea. The sea his father had abandoned, and the mother that had abandoned him. He'd often sat in the cleft in the rock and wondered about that. He always started by thinking about what was least difficult to face up to.

The sea.

If his father had been forced to abandon ship, how come that he was washed up in this little town in the north of Sweden where there wasn't even any sea? And how could he find any satisfaction in going into the forest every day to chop down trees when he'd never succeed in felling enough for him to be able to glimpse the open sea beyond?

How can you be washed up in a place where there isn't even any sea?

How can you drift ashore in the middle of a vast, dark forest?

What had really happened? Why did they have to live here, in the middle of this vast, dark forest, so far away from the sea?

Samuel, his father, was born in Bohuslän in the south-west of Sweden, he knew that. Right next to the sea, in a fisherman's cottage to the north of Marstrand. But why had Joel been born in Sundsvall, in the north-east of Sweden?

Mum, he thought. She's at the bottom of it all. The woman who didn't want to stay with them. The woman who one day packed a suitcase and took a train heading south when his dad was out in the forest, working.

Joel didn't know how old he was at the time. All he knew was that he'd been too young to remember anything.

But old Mrs Westman on the ground floor had told him. One day he'd managed to lock himself out and it was twenty degrees below freezing and his dad wouldn't be back home for several hours. She'd invited him into her flat to wait. It was dark there, and smelt of winter apples and acrid candles.

Mrs Westman was old and hunchbacked. He'd once seen her lose her false teeth when she had a sneezing fit in the garden. The whole of her dingy flat was full of pictures of God. There was even a picture of Jesus on the doormat. The first time he'd been there, or at least the first time he could remember, he didn't know where to put his boots to dry—they were covered in dirty snow.

'Stand them on the doormat,' said

Mrs Westman. 'He knows what you're thinking and He's watching you wherever you go. So why shouldn't He be on a doormat?'

She let Joel sit on a reindeer pelt she'd spread out in front of the open fire in the kitchen. He couldn't remember how old he was then, but suddenly she'd bent down over him with her hunched back.

'There were no evil intentions in your mum,' she said. 'But she had a restlessness inside her. I could see that as soon as they moved here, Samuel and your mum. She was always itching to be somewhere else. She came down with you one day and asked if you could stay with me until your dad came home. She had an errand to see to, she said. But I could see she was restless, and I'd noticed the suitcase she'd left outside the door. But I don't think there were any evil intentions in her. It was just the itch inside her, whether she liked it or not . . .'

Joel can sit in the crack in his rock down by the river and carefully join together one thought after another until suddenly everything becomes clear.

He has a father called Samuel who longs for the sea.

He has a mother who had something called an Itch.

Sometimes when his dad looks at him and his eyes seem especially gloomy, Joel lies in bed worrying, waiting for the clinking of a bottle in the kitchen when Samuel thinks he's fallen asleep. He tiptoes to the door and looks through the keyhole into the kitchen. His dad sits on the kitchen bench mumbling away, stroking his hand through his shaggy hair over and over again. He keeps taking deep swigs from the bottle, as if he'd prefer not to, but he can't help it.

Why doesn't he pour some into a glass? Joel wonders.

Why does he drink something that seems to taste so awful?

One morning when Joel wakes up, his dad has fallen asleep at the kitchen table. His head is slumped down on the table top, and his clenched fist is resting on a sea chart.

But there's something else on the blue oilcloth table cover.

A photograph, creased and well-thumbed, with one corner torn off. It's a photograph of a woman. A woman with brown hair, looking straight at Joel.

He knows immediately that it's his mother gazing at him.

She's not smiling nor scowling. Just looking at him, and he thinks that is what somebody with an Itch looks like.

It says Jenny on the back. And there's the name of a photo studio in Sundsvall.

Jenny. Samuel and Jenny and Joel Gustafson. If they'd been a family, that's what they'd have been called.

Now they are just names that don't fit together. Joel thinks he must ask his father what really happened.

Not now, not today, but some other day when there isn't an empty bottle on the kitchen table when he gets up to go to school. Not until his dad has given the kitchen a good scrubbing and everything has settled down. One of these nights when the kitchen has been cleaned up he'll be able to start talking to his father again.

It always happens at night.

He's woken up by the noise coming from the kitchen. There is a clanging and clanking of pots and pans. His father is muttering and hissing and roaring with laughter, much too loudly. That tells Joel he's started scrubbing down the kitchen.

He gets out of bed and watches him through the half-open kitchen door.

Samuel is splattering water all over the floor and the walls. Steam is rising from the glowing stove and his face is sweaty and shiny. He's scrubbing away like mad at stains and specks of dirt that only he can see. He throws a whole bucketful of sizzling water into the hood over the stove. He squelches around the floor in his soaking wet woollen socks and scrubs so hard, it seems that doing so relieves him of a great pain.

Joel can't make up his mind if his dad is scared or if he's angry.

What kind of dirt is it that he can see, but nobody else can?

He can hear Samuel muttering and chuntering about spiders' webs and clusters of snakes. But surely there aren't any spiders making webs in the kitchen in the middle of winter? And how could there be a cluster of snakes in the hood over the stove? There aren't any snakes at all in this part of northern Sweden.

Joel watches him through the half-open door and realises that his father is scrubbing away something that only he can see. Something that makes him both scared and angry.

When Samuel has finished, he lies on his bed without moving. He groans and doesn't open the curtains even though it's broad daylight. He's still on the bed when Joel goes to school, and he's still there when Joel comes back home in the afternoon.

When Joel has boiled the potatoes and asks his father if he wants to eat, he just groans and shakes his head. A few days later everything is back to normal, as if it had simply been a dream. His father gets up at five o'clock again, has his coffee and goes off into the forest. Joel can breathe freely again. It will be a long time before he's woken up by his father sitting at the kitchen table muttering away to himself.

It's easiest to think about all the things that happen and make him wonder what's going on when he's sitting in the crack in his rock down by the river.

One day he sits down at the kitchen table with a pen and some paper and writes down all the things he thinks about. He lists the questions he's going to ask his father. Questions he wants answering before the first snow has fallen in the autumn. When he writes down his questions it's still the middle of winter. There are big mounds of snow thrown up by the ploughs at street corners and by the wall of the church. It's bitterly cold when he goes to school in the morning. But spring will come one of these days.

His first question will be why they don't live by the sea.

That might not be the most important question, but he wants to start with something that isn't too hard.

For every question he writes down, he also tries to work out what possible answers there might be, and what answer he would most like to hear.

Then he wants to know why he was born in Sundsvall.

And why Jenny, his mother, went off in a train and left him with Mrs Westman.

That's also difficult because he never knows what to say whenever anybody asks him why he doesn't have a mother.

He's the only one. The only person he knows who doesn't have a mother.

Being the only one can often be a good thing.

Being the only one with a model aeroplane made of balsa wood, or having a bike with a steel-studded tyre on the back wheel.

But being the only one without a mother is a bad thing.

It's worse than wearing glasses.

It's even worse than stuttering.

Being without a mother is the worst

thing there is.

The only mum allowed not to be there is a mum who's died.

He sometimes thinks he will give that answer when somebody asks, or is taunting him. He's tested it to hear what it sounds like.

'My mum died.'

But there are lots of ways of saying that. You can say it to make it sound as if she died in a dramatic plane crash in some far distant country, when she was on some urgent mission. Or you can say it to suggest that she was attacked by a lion.

'My mother's dead' is another way he could say it.

That makes it sound as if he doesn't really care.

But when he finds the photograph that morning, when his dad's asleep with his head on the kitchen table, he knows that his mother isn't dead. And he knows that he has to find out what happened.

Every night before he goes to sleep he thinks up a story with her in it, something he can lie and fantasise about before he dozes off. The one he likes best is when he imagines she is a figurehead on the bows of a ship with three tall masts and lots of billowing sails.

Sometimes he's the captain of the ship, sometimes it's his father. They always very nearly capsize but manage to make their way through the submerged rocks and sandbanks in the end. It's a good dream because he can think up lots of different endings.

But sometimes when he's in a bad mood he allows the ship to sink and the figurehead is buried two thousand fathoms deep. The exhausted crew manage to scramble onto a desert island, but he lets Jenny, his mother, disappear for ever at the bottom of the sea.

Samuel Island or Joel Island. The desert island they eventually land on is never called Jenny Island.

It's usually when he's been annoyed by Otto that he lets the ship sink.

Even if he's generally on his guard, always ready for somebody in the school playground to start asking awkward questions, Otto has a way of creeping up on him on the sly and catching him out when he's forgotten to have an answer ready.

Otto is older than Joel and is repeating a year because he has some illness or other and nobody understands what it is. Sometimes he's off school for months on end, and if he misses any more this year he'll have to repeat the year yet again. Otto's father is a fireman with the railway, and if you're lucky you can go with Otto and see what goes on in the engine sheds.

But Joel isn't one of those allowed to go along. He and Otto are usually at each other's throats.

'If I'd have been a mum and had a son like you, I'd have run away as well,' says Otto out of the blue, loud enough for everybody in the school yard to hear.

Joel doesn't know what to say.

'My mum's a figurehead,' he says. 'But I don't suppose you know what that is.'

The answer he hasn't prepared at all seems to be a good one, because Otto

24

doesn't respond.

The next time I'll hold my tongue and just thump him one, Joel thinks. I'm bound to get beaten up because he's older and bigger than me. But maybe I'll be able to bite him . . .

The next class is geography. Miss Nederström emerges from the staff room where she makes tea and solves crossword puzzles during the lesson breaks. She has a club foot and she's been Joel's teacher ever since he started school.

Once he put on an act to amuse the rest of the pupils by walking behind her, imitating her limp.

She suddenly turned round and smiled.

'You're very good,' she said. 'That's exactly how I walk.'

If she hadn't had a club foot Joel could well imagine having her as a mum. But Miss Nederström is in fact a Mrs and has children of her own with the surveyor she's married to.

Geography is Joel's best subject. He never forgets what his father tells him, and he has a diary with maps of all the countries of the world in it. He knows where Pamplemousse and Bogamaio are, although he's not at all sure how to pronounce them.

Nobody else in the class knows as much about the world as Joel. Perhaps he doesn't know all that much about Sweden, but he knows more than anybody else about what lies beyond the dark forests and over the sea.

No sooner have they sat down than Otto puts his hand up. Joel doesn't realise he's done so because Otto sits in the row behind him.

Miss Nederström nods at him.

'Do you want to go home?' she asks. 'Don't you feel well?'

Otto rarely puts his hand up unless he's feeling ill. But this time he has a question.

'What is a figural head?' he asks.

Joel gives a start and feels his heart beginning to pound. He might have known. That bastard Otto! He's going to be shown up now. Everybody heard what he said about his mother being a figurehead.

'Come again,' said Miss Nederström.

'What did you say it was?'

'A figural head,' said Otto again.

'No, it's called a figurehead,' said Miss Nederström.

Don't tell him, thought Joel. Don't tell him . . .

And she doesn't.

'Is there anybody in the class who knows what a figurehead is?' she asks.

Nobody answers, least of all Joel, the only one who knows.

Then Otto puts his hand up again.

'Joel knows,' he said. 'His mum is a figural . . . one of those things . . .'

Miss Nederström looks at Joel.

'Where on earth did you get that from?' she said. 'A figurehead is a wooden carving attached to the bows of a ship. Not nowadays, but in the old days when they had sailing ships. Nobody can have a mum made of wood.'

Joel has time to swear that he hates both Miss Nederström and Otto before the whole class bursts into cruel laughter.

'You know a lot about all kinds of unusual things,' says Miss Nederström,

27

'but I must say you sometimes get carried away by your imagination.'

Joel stares down at his desk lid, feels his face turning red, and he hates and hates as hard as he can.

'Joel,' says Miss Nederström. 'Look at me!'

He slowly raises his head that feels as heavy as a block of stone.

'There's nothing wrong with having imagination and making things up,' she says, 'but you must distinguish between what is fantasy and what is real. You remember that time about the water-lilies?'

The water lilies! Of course he remembers, even though he's been trying to forget. The outsize water lilies on Mauritius that his father had once told him about. As big as the centre circle of the ice-hockey pitch they create every winter on the flat, sandy space outside the school by spraying water onto it and allowing it to freeze—the temperature never rises above zero, and they can play on it for months.

One day everybody in the class was

asked to talk about something exciting they'd read about or heard somebody talking about.

Joel had told the story of the water lilies on Mauritius.

'I don't suppose they are really as big as that,' Miss Nederström had said when he'd finished his piece.

He had been silly enough to insist he was right.

'They are as big as that,' he said. 'Maybe even bigger.'

'Who told you that?' asked Miss Nederström.

'My dad saw them when he was a sailor,' said Joel, 'and he bloody well knows what he's talking about.'

He didn't know where the swearword had come from. But Miss Nederström was angry and sent him out of the classroom.

After that he'd made up his mind never to say anything about far-distant lands again in class. How are they supposed to know what reality looks like? All they've ever seen is snow and the endless forests.

He trudges home from school

through the snow flurries. It's started to get dark already even though it's only early afternoon.

I'm eleven years old now, he thought. One of these days I'll be an old man, and eventually I shall die. But by then I'll be a long way away from here, a long way away from all this snow and that Otto who can never keep his mouth shut.

His nose is running, and he hurries on home.

He collects a kilo of potatoes from Svenson's, the grocer's; a pack of butter and a loaf of bread. Svenson, who's never fully sober and has grease stains on his jacket, notes the items down in his notebook.

I go shopping like a bloody mum, he thought angrily. First I buy the goods on tick, then I boil the potatoes. I'm like a mother to myself.

As he passes through the garden gate, hanging skewwhiff from its hinges, it dawns on him that this house will never float away down the river. There will never be a suitable wind. It might have been better to smash the house up, like his dad had told him they did to old tubs past their sell-by date.

He runs up the dark, creaking staircase, opens the door to their flat and lights a fire in the stove before he's even started to take his boots off.

Something has to happen, he thinks. I don't want to wait any longer.

While the potatoes are boiling he searches tentatively through his dad's room for the photograph of his mum, Jenny. He sifts through books and clothes, and all the rolled-up sea charts, but he doesn't find anything.

Has he taken the photo into the forest with him? he wonders. Why is he keeping it from me?

He decides to ask his father that the moment he comes home, before he's even had time to take off his woolly hat.

It's my mum after all, he thinks. Why is he keeping her from me?

But when he hears his father's footsteps coming up the stairs, he knows he isn't going to ask him anything.

He daren't. Instead he asks his dad to repeat the story about the enormous water lilies that only exist in the botanical gardens in Mauritius.

Samuel sits down on the edge of Joel's bed.

'Wouldn't you rather hear about something else?' he asks. 'I've told you about the water lilies so many times.'

'Not tonight,' Joel tells him. 'Tonight I want to hear something I've heard about before.'

Afterwards he lies down in the dark, listening to the beams twisting and creaking.

Something's got to happen, he tells himself before he dozes off with the sheets pulled up to his chin.

He suddenly wakes up in the middle of the night. And that's when, as he gets out of bed and tiptoes over to the window, he sees that solitary dog running off towards the stars.

3

There are two things Joel Gustafson wants.

A new stove and a bicycle.

He can't quite make up his mind which of those is the more important. He realises that two things can never be equally important at the same time, but he's unsure when it comes to choosing between the stove and the bicycle.

He knows of nobody apart from himself and his father who cook food on an old iron, wood-burning stove. Everybody has an electric cooker nowadays. Nobody but him has to chop up kindling, carry in firewood and wait for ever and a day until the so-called hotplates have heated up sufficiently to boil the water for the potatoes.

It is a real pain, having to stand by the stove every day after school, making sure the fire doesn't go out. That's the kind of thing people used to have to do. Not now, though, not in the spring of 1956.

One day he plucks up enough courage to ask his father.

The wood had been damp and wouldn't ignite. In addition, he'd burnt himself on the pan when the potatoes were finally ready.

'Don't you think we should get rid of this old stove?' he says.

Samuel looks up from the kitchen bench, where he's lying down and thumbing through a newspaper.

'What's wrong with the stove?' he asks. 'Has it cracked?'

What's wrong with it? Joel asks himself. Everything is wrong with it. The biggest thing wrong with it is that it's not an electric cooker.

'Everybody has an electric cooker,' he says. 'Everybody but us.'

His father peers at him over his reading glasses.

'How many people do you think have a model ship called *Celestine*?' he asks. 'How many apart from us? Should we get rid of that as well? So that we are like everybody else?'

Joel doesn't like it when his dad

answers a question by asking another one. That makes it hard to stick to the point that really matters. But this time he's going to be insistent.

'If I'm going to have to carry on boiling potatoes, I want an electric cooker,' he says.

Then he says something he hadn't intended to say at all.

'If I'm the mother in this household.'

His father turns serious, and looks at him long and hard without responding.

Joel wishes he could read his father's thoughts.

'An electric cooker is quite expensive,' says Samuel in the end. 'But we'll buy one as soon as I've saved up enough money. I promise. If that's how you feel.'

At that moment Joel loves his father. Only somebody who's been a sailor understands immediately what you mean, he thinks. Only somebody who's learnt how to make important decisions while terrible storms are raging on the seven seas understands when it's time to throw out an old wood-burning stove.

At the same time he's a bit sorry he didn't start by mentioning the bicycle. Now it's too late. Now he'll have to wait with that for a few weeks at least. You can't ask for two things at the same time, that's one thing too many.

He works it out in his head.

Today is March 3rd. He won't be able to get a bike for at least a month. But there will still be snow everywhere and it would be impossible to ride it. That's good. That means he wouldn't need to be the last boy in the school with no bicycle. But he ought to have mentioned the electric cooker much earlier. I must remember that in future, he thinks. Never wait too long before asking for something.

But more important than both the cooker and the bike is the dog.

The night Joel asked his dad about the electric cooker, he lies in bed unable to sleep. He can hear the radio that Samuel is listening to through the wall. There's still music playing. If he's still awake when the pips sound before the news, he'll be very tired when he has to get up for school tomorrow

36

morning.

He listens to the cold that is making the walls creak. The rafters are groaning and sighing. Soon the days will grow longer and lighter. The snowdrifts will melt away, just as they always do. The first cowslips will eventually appear, glowing yellow by the side of the road.

Joel decides to go looking for the dog.

If it hasn't yet reached a star, I shall find it, he thinks.

He decides to go looking for the dog during the night. Night after night when his dad has fallen asleep, he'll get up, get dressed and sneak out into the darkness.

Perhaps everything is different at night-time. Perhaps the dog is only visible at night. Just think, there might be Day People and Night People. People who are only visible at night. Children who go to school at night. Parents who chop down trees in the forest or go out shopping. Night People and Night Schools, Night Cars and Night Houses, Night Churches and a Night Sun. Not the moon, but a real sun that is only visible to the people who live during the night.

He can hear that the late news has started on the radio. Samuel has turned up the volume because he no doubt thinks Joel will be asleep now. In fact Joel is wide awake, lying in his bed and waiting for his dad to drop off to sleep before getting up and going out into the night.

This is how an adventure ought to start. An adventure you create for yourself, that you are the only person involved in . . .

The news comes to an end and Joel hears his dad switch off the radio and go out into the kitchen to get washed.

Joel knows exactly what his dad does. First he washes his face, then he brushes his teeth, and then he gargles. When he switches the light off in the kitchen he usually clears his throat.

Joel waits impatiently for everything to go quiet. But before he realises what's happening he falls asleep, and when he wakes up it's morning and his father has already disappeared into the forest.

Joel is tired and annoyed when he forces himself to get out of bed. The cork floor tiles never feel as cold as they do when he hasn't had enough sleep. Moreover his buttonholes are too small and his socks too tight, and he hits his head on the hood over the stove when he tries to warm his hands.

He has often wondered what actually happens when he falls asleep. He's tried imagining a little creature wandering about inside him, snuffing out a series of wax candles, and when it's completely dark, he's asleep. It will be one of those Night People, he thinks.

They want to be left in peace during the night. They want us to sleep.

He doesn't really want to go to school today. He would prefer to creep back into bed and go back to sleep, so that he's properly rested when night comes. He doesn't want to miss out on his newly thought-up adventure yet again.

But he puts on his rubber boots and clears the stairs in four jumps. He's made up his mind that before his twelfth birthday he will get to the bottom in three hops.

When he turns off by the church he starts running so as not to be late. Miss Nederström doesn't like her pupils arriving late. If you do, you have to stand up and explain why. And then there's the risk of Otto marching up to you at break asking why your mother didn't wake you up in time.

He takes a short cut along the white paths through the churchyard, taking a quick look round to see if there are any new graves. As usual he jumps over a black headstone where it says 'The Family Grave of Nils Wiberg, Farmer of this Parish', but it's icy underneath the snow today and he slips and hurts his bottom.

Ghosts exist even though he doesn't believe in them. Perhaps it's Nils Wiberg who doesn't like the idea of Joel jumping over his grave?

He races over the schoolyard and gets to the top of the stairs just in time.

The school bell is ringing and he imagines that it is the captain of the barque *Celestine* summoning his crew to their stations. This very day in 1956 they will set sail from Bristol and head for Biscay with a cargo of live horses and some cloth from a textile mill in Manchester.

Just like his father had told him about. Heading for Biscay with horses and fabrics.

On the way home from school Joel calls in at the bookshop and buys a little notebook for two kronor. He has nineteen kronor stashed away in a tin under his bed. He uses two of those coins to buy a book in which he can write down all the things he is sure are going to happen.

Logbook, he knows that's what it's called. Every ship has a logbook. Every day the skipper notes down what winds are blowing, the location of the vessel and anything unusual that has happened. If a ship gets into difficulties, the logbook always has to be rescued.

'It's the ship's Bible,' his dad told

him. 'It tells the history of the vessel.'

While he's waiting for the potatoes to boil, he sits down at the kitchen table with his notebook and a pencil in front of him.

'The Search For The Dog That Headed For A Star', he writes on the cover. He underlines the first letter of every word and inserts a few vowels so that he can pronounce it. THESEFOTHEDOTHFAS.

That's the code for a secret society of course, he thinks. A secret society whose name nobody will be able to guess. He starts writing on the first page.

'The search for the dog that headed for a star began on March 8, 1956. The weather was fine. Clear sky, plus four degrees, colder towards evening.' He reads what he has written and has the feeling that the adventure is now under way. It's already there inside him. When you have an adventure inside you the only thing that matters is what happens next. Just as on a ship like the *Celestine*.

The figurehead on the bows always

looks ahead. Never backwards.

He suddenly has an idea.

He will hide the logbook in the *Celestine*'s display case. If he lifts the model up carefully he can put the book underneath her so that nobody can see it. Of course that's where the logbook ought to be!

The evening passes so unbearably slowly. Joel lies down on his bed and tries to read a book, but he can't concentrate. He fetches a needle and thread and tries to darn a hole in his sock. He can usually do this rather well, but tonight the thread gets tangled and he has to cut it away. He goes into his father's room and sits with him, listening to the radio.

A man with a high-pitched voice is going on about how important it is for cows to have enough space in their stalls.

He glances at Samuel, who is sitting in his worn-out armchair with his eyes closed.

Is he really listening to this? Joel wonders. Surely he's not interested in cows?

Suddenly it seems as if his dad has read Joel's thoughts.

'You forgot to buy milk from Mr Svenson today,' he said. 'Don't forget tomorrow.'

If the adventure and the secret society are not going to be exposed, it's important that he doesn't forget anything. Everything has to be exactly the same as usual.

'I won't forget tomorrow,' he says. 'I'll get some milk tomorrow.'

'It's getting late,' says his dad. 'Time to go to bed.'

Joel creeps into bed and lies waiting.

When the news has finished, Joel can hear his father gargling. He can see through the crack in the door when the light goes out. There are some creaking noises from the bed, then all is quiet. He waits for a bit longer before getting dressed. He knows there is a loose floorboard in the kitchen but even so he treads in the wrong place and makes a creaking noise.

He holds his breath and listens hard in the darkness.

Samuel hasn't heard anything.

Joel carefully opens the front door with his boots and jacket in his hand, and sneaks out into the vestibule. He laces up his boots, buttons up his jacket and pulls his woolly hat down over his ears. He's ready now. The secret society THESEFOTHE DOTHFAS has embarked on its journey out into the unknown ...

When he emerges into the open it's cold and totally still. The weak streetlamps cast a yellow glow over the piled-up snow. He cautiously makes his way out through the gate and looks round. He can hear a car in the distance. He stands absolutely still until the engine noise has died away.

Then he starts walking through the deserted little town. For no special reason he finds himself taking the route he usually follows when going to school. But everything is different at night.

He has the feeling that the black houses, the shuttered windows, are looking at him, not the other way round. And his boots are making a very loud crunching noise in the cold snow. He stops outside the Grand Hotel and watches a cat climbing over the fence to Franzen's garage. But there is no sign of any people. Not until he's passing Hultman's shoe shop does he hear some people laughing from behind a lit-up window on the second floor.

It feels comforting to know that he's not entirely on his own.

He allows the laughing people to become members of his secret society.

They'll never know anything about it, but they can't stop me letting them join it.

He walks back through the town, down towards the river and the railway bridge with its enormous iron arches. He walks along one of the rails until he's in the middle of the bridge. He leans over the parapet and looks down at the ice below. Then he looks up at the sky. There are no clouds and he can see the stars glimmering like candles up above him.

If I were to climb up one of the arches, I'd get closer to them, he thinks.

He decides to introduce a hero's rule. Nobody can be a full member of the secret society, not even he, until they've climbed over one of the arches.

He's starting to feel cold and tired. He hasn't even thought about looking for the dog. But he has plenty of nights ahead of him. Besides, it will soon be spring, and the nights will get warmer and lighter.

He finds a stone by the railway track and throws it over the parapet and onto the ice down below. Then he goes home.

This first night he's only done a bit of reconnoitring. Tomorrow night is when he'll start looking for the dog, start out on the great adventure.

He tiptoes up the stairs, unlaces his boots and carefully opens the flat door. If Samuel has woken up, Joel has no idea how he's going to explain away his nocturnal wandering.

He listens outside the door, but all is quiet. Dad's asleep.

He quickly gets undressed, creeps into bed and curls up in order to get warm. He thinks about what to write in the logbook tomorrow. 'The first night Joel Gustafson completed his reconnaissance mission to everyone's complete satisfaction. The adventure has begun. The dog has not yet been tracked down.'

Then he falls asleep and when he wakes up next morning he doesn't feel tired at all. Hurrying to school and thinking about how he'd gone the same way in the middle of the night is really a big deal.

Tonight, he thinks. Tonight I shall find the dog that's heading for a star . . .

*   *   *

The next night when Joel sets off on his adventure, everything starts to go wrong. In the dark kitchen he trips up over his own boots and knocks a saucepan off the stove as he falls. He thinks it sounds as if the ceiling had come crashing down when the saucepan hits the floor. He rushes back into his room and jumps into bed with all his clothes still on and pulls the

48

cover up to his chin.

That must have woken his father up, he thinks. Nobody could have slept through that row. Least of all a sailor. But not a sound comes from his dad's room. He's still asleep. He hasn't heard a thing. Joel gets up once more.

Back in the kitchen he gropes around for the saucepan. It's ended up in a corner, between the sofa and the firewood bin. Joel places it carefully on the table, then goes out into the hall carrying his boots and jacket.

When he's outside in the street, listening to the silence, it occurs to him that there's something badly wrong with the secret society he's founded.

The word society means that there's more than one person involved. Joel on his own can't be a society.

But who can he ask to join? Who could he possibly share his secret with?

Joel has a lot of friends, but none of them is sufficiently close for him to share his secret with him.

If only I had a brother, he thinks. If Mum was determined to run away, the least she could have done would have been to leave me a brother.

He suddenly felt sad.

'Why should I go running around on my own in the middle of the night, looking for a dog that might not exist?' he asks himself aloud.

Just as he says that it starts snowing. A few snowflakes dance around under the streetlight. Then there are more and more, and he thinks crossly that spring is going to be delayed this year as well. The only good thing about it starting to snow is that he might be able to get a bicycle before everybody else has started cycling around.

He decides to take a look at the new bikes on display in the cycle shop window, before starting to look for the dog. There's a particular one he wants to see. It has a red frame and there's a logo with a flying horse just above the pump holder.

He hears a car coming and sees its headlights in the distance. He stands in the shadow cast by the tall gatepost next to the chemist's. When the vehicle passes he sees that it is in fact the rusty old lorry belonging to The Old

Bricklayer.

He has an odd name, Joel remembers that. Simon Windstorm. But he's never referred to as anything but The Old Bricklayer. Everybody is a bit scared of him. He was once locked up in a home for madmen. Joel knows he was in there for nearly ten years. Nobody thought he would ever get out, but one day he jumped off the train at the local station and explained that he'd been released because he was fit again.

But why is he driving his lorry around in the middle of the night?

Joel presses on and thinks he must make a note of The Old Bricklayer in his logbook. It's something special that has to be recorded.

Anton Wiberg's bicycle shop is on the corner of Norra Vägen and Kyrkogatan. Joel pauses in the shadows before approaching the display window. There are a lot of streetlamps and illuminated shop windows just there. If he stands in front of the window anybody could see him. He checks the blocks of flats on all sides, but it's dark in all those windows.

He runs quickly over the street, jumps over the heaped-up snow left in the gutter by the snow plough, and there's the red bike. The Flying Horse.

There are a lot of bicycles in the window, but it's only the red one that interests Joel. That's the one he wants to be riding this spring.

He's been into the shop several times and asked about the price, and he knows it is only slightly more expensive than the rest of the bikes. The hard part won't be persuading his father to buy him that particular one, but getting a bicycle at all. It takes his father a long time to make up his mind about things, but once he's decided, fifty kronor is neither here nor there.

But there is another danger as well.

Anton Wiberg has only one red bicycle. There are several of all the other models. He must make sure nobody gets there before him and buys the red bike.

Joel pictures Otto in his mind's eye, coming towards him on the red bike.

It's a horrible thought he would rather not entertain.

The trouble is that Samuel always takes such a long time to make up his mind. When there is only one red bicycle, he has to get a move on.

Joel takes one last look at the bike, then goes round to the back of the building for a pee.

A single bulb in a broken shade is shining over the back door. Joel pees into the snow and tries to write his name. It's not hard to write Joel, but he never has enough for more than half the surname. He kicks some snow over the yellow letters and refastens his fly. Without really knowing why, he walks up to the back door and tries it. Perhaps he's afraid that somebody might try to steal The Flying Horse.

To his astonishment he discovers that the door is unlocked. He can see right into the shop. See the bikes in the illuminated display window. The counter and the cash register.

His heart is pounding as Joel does what he really doesn't dare to do.

He closes the door behind him,

tiptoes past the counter and goes to the bike that one day will be his.

There's a nice smell of oil and rubber. The saddle is wrapped up in paper. To keep it clean.

I'm not going to think at all, he tells himself. I'm simply going to do what I want to do but don't really dare.

He slowly removes the bicycle from its place in the window display and wheels it towards the back door. He cautiously opens the door and peers out. It's almost stopped snowing. He carries the bike down the steps, switches on the dynamo on the front wheel, then pedals off. He turns into Norra Vägen, where the sanded road surface hasn't yet been covered in newly-fallen snow. And he keeps on going.

When he gets to the Hedevägen crossroads he stops and listens for traffic, but all is quiet and he sets off again. It's hard not to think. Not to be scared stiff of what he's doing.

I've become a Petty Thief, he thinks as he climbs the hill leading to the railway station. A Petty Thief who can't keep his hands off what isn't his.

He tries to calm himself down with the thought that he had no intention of stealing the bicycle, merely of trying it out.

Maybe he ought to write a note to Anton Wiberg and pin it to the door? Saying that The Secret Society's night patrol has discovered a back door unlocked and been keeping a lookout for Petty Thieves all night long . . .

He climbs up the hill to the railway station and is concentrating so hard on not falling over and damaging the bike that he forgets to listen out for cars.

Suddenly, out of nowhere, two headlights are coming straight at him. He gives a start and swerves towards the side of the road.

Now I'm done for, he thinks in desperation. I've nowhere to hide.

The front wheel skids into the snow piled up in the gutter and before he knows where he is, he falls over and the bike lands on top of him in the snow. He can hear the car pulling up behind him, a door opening, then winter boots squelching in the snow.

It's Dad, he thinks. I didn't mean it. I wasn't going to steal it, I was just going to . . .

'Are you all right?' he hears a voice saying.

When he looks up he sees The Old Bricklayer standing over him, his woolly hat pulled down over his ears.

'Have you hurt yourself?' he asks. 'What on earth are you doing at this time of night, cycling around town?'

Joel feels a strong arm pulling him up out of the snowdrift.

Simon Windstorm is mad, he thinks. He's going to kill me.

'You seem to be OK,' says Windstorm. 'Go back home to bed now! I won't insist on knowing what you're doing out here at this time. That's none of my business. Me, I drive around at night in my lorry because I can't get to sleep. Off you go now!'

The Old Bricklayer mutters something to himself then goes back to his lorry and drives away. Joel wheels the bike back to the shop as quickly as he can. He carries it up the steps,

56

opens the back door and puts it back in the display window. He tries to wipe it clean with his woolly hat, but the frame is scratched in one place and he can't do anything about that. He expects Anton Wiberg to appear beside him at any moment.

I'm out of my mind, he thinks and can feel himself starting to cry with fear. He rubs and rubs. The bike will never be clean and dry again.

Just at that very moment he looks out of the window, into the deserted street.

There comes the dog!

The solitary dog heading for a star.

Joel knows right away that it's the very same dog. There's no other dog like it, even if it seems to be just an ordinary Norwegian elkhound.

Suddenly it stops and looks round.

Just for a moment Joel thinks it's looking straight at him, through the shop window.

Then it sets off running again.

Joel rushes out through the back door, trips up on the steps and falls headfirst.

When he gets to the street the dog has disappeared. The street is deserted. He goes to the streetlight, but there's no sign of any pawprints. No sign of any dog.

Joel sets off running through the night, and it's started snowing again.

Back in bed he thinks about the dog he's seen. The dog really was there, he'd seen it. Perhaps a dog heading for a star doesn't leave any tracks behind it.

His fear gradually fades away. The Old Bricklayer can't know that the bike Joel had ridden into the snow had been pinched. And nobody will be able to find his name peed into the snow. By the time he wakes up the yellow marks will have been covered over. I'll get away with it, he thinks.

But the dog does exist. And the adventure, the great adventure has begun . . .

4

A few days later Joel fell asleep at his desk in school.

He had no idea how it came about. All of a sudden he was just sitting there with his mouth open, fast asleep.

It was an RE class, and Miss Nederström was red in the face with anger when she shook him by the shoulder to wake him up.

She had a patch of eczema on her forehead, just under her hair line. When her face turned red and the spots became white, everybody knew that she was furious.

'Joel,' she bellowed. 'Joel Gustafson! How dare you sleep through my lesson!'

He woke up with a start. He'd been dreaming something that vanished the moment he woke up. Something about his father. In the dream Joel had been in a vast forest, looking for him, but that was all he could remember.

When he woke up he couldn't believe

that he'd been asleep. Asleep at his desk?

'No,' he said. 'I wasn't asleep.'

'Don't sit there telling me barefaced lies. You were asleep. The whole class could see that.'

Joel looked round. He was surrounded by embarrassed faces, grinning faces, curious faces.

Faces that told him Miss Nederström was telling the truth. He had fallen asleep.

He was ordered to leave the room, and Miss Nederström said she would be phoning his father.

Joel didn't respond.

She could find out for herself that they didn't have a telephone.

He sat on the floor in the empty corridor, eyeing all the shoes lined up against the wall. He thought he might get his own back on all those grinning faces by mixing the shoes up. Or throwing them out into the yard. But he decided not to.

Instead he took The Secret Society logbook out of his pocket. He'd forgotten to put it in *Celestine*'s glass case that morning.

He searched through the jackets hanging in the corridor until he found a pen, then started writing.

'The lookout on the mizzen mast, Joel Gustafson, was so exhausted that he fell out of his crow's nest, but survived without serious injury. After resting for merely a couple of hours, he was ready to climb up the mast once more.'

What he writes is almost word-for-word something he'd read in a book his dad keeps in his little bookcase, and often thumbs through. That's the kind of thing you put in a secret logbook, Joel thinks.

Only somebody with inside information can know that it's really about him being thrown out of the classroom.

It's not good, being sent out like that. Better than wearing glasses or stuttering, but not good whichever way you look at it.

Joel can put up with his classmates grinning at him. So long as you don't start blushing or crying when you're sent out of the room, you are an important person.

What is not so good is that Miss Nederström might come and visit them once she discovers that the Gustafsons don't have a telephone. If that happens, Joel might have a lot of awkward questions to answer. His father might start to suspect that Joel goes out at night. He tries to think of a good way of solving the problem, but he can't. There are only bad solutions. Like staying behind after school and knocking on the staffroom door and asking to speak to Miss Nederström, and then apologising and explaining that he'd been awake all night with toothache. It's a bad solution because it's a cowardly way out.

Joel keeps on thinking.

Maybe he ought to take the cowardly way out after all. The main thing is that his father shouldn't start getting suspicious.

When the bell rings and the lesson is over, Joel decides to take the cowardly way out. He is responsible for the secret society, and he doesn't want to run the risk of not being able to find that solitary dog.

When he knocks on the staffroom door after school, Miss Nederström believes every word he tells her. Instead of saying he had toothache, he says he had stomach ache. If you have toothache there is a risk that you might end up having to go to the dentist.

'It's good that you have come to explain,' she says. 'Now we can forget all about it. But you do understand that I was very cross when I noticed that you were asleep, don't you?'

'Yes, Miss,' says Joel.

Slush is sloshing all round his boots as he walks home.

One day it snows, the next day it thaws.

Joel hopes that spring will soon be here, but he knows it could just as easily turn very wintry again. The first year he started school, it snowed on the last day of term at the beginning of June. He remembered having holes in his shoes and snow melted inside them, and he burst out sneezing when Miss Nederström asked him a question.

Joel is not sure whether or not he dares to walk past the cycle shop. Maybe it will be obvious from looking at him that he'd been out that night with The Flying Horse? Or perhaps he might faint as he walks past?

He's scared of fainting, even though he's never done it. But he often imagines collapsing in a heap when he's said something that isn't true, or done something he ought not to do.

What frightens him most of all, though, is that he might give himself away. That he might stop outside the shop and shout that he was the one who borrowed the red bike one night when he discovered that the back door was unlocked. There's nothing that scares Joel more that him being unable to stop himself doing something. Not being responsible for his own actions.

He stops outside Leander Nilson's bakery and looks at the window. It's not the cakes he's examining, but his own reflection. In amongst all the buns and cakes is a mirror, and he can see his face in it.

Not that there's all that much to see. He has his woolly hat pulled well down over his forehead, and his scarf above his chin. But although he can only see his eyes, his nose and his mouth, he feels he can see his whole face even so.

He's not pleased with what he sees.

What is worst is that he thinks he looks like a girl.

He can't make up his mind why. Besides, nobody has ever told him he looks like a girl. He's the only one who thinks he has a face like a girl's.

The only bit he thinks is good is his nose. It's not too big and not too small. It's straight, doesn't have any lumps and it's not turned up. There's no chance of it snowing into Joel Gustafson's nose.

He'd prefer to exchange the rest of his face. Green eyes are nothing worth having. His mouth is too thin and his left ear juts out. His hair is black but it ought to have been fair, or at least brown.

He also has a crown over his forehead which makes his hair stand up like a fan after it's been cut. His father cuts his hair, and he always clips it too short.

You ought to be able to choose for yourself what you look like, he thinks. Go through some photographs and say: 'That's how I want to be!'

What annoys him most of all is that he doesn't look like his dad at all. That must mean that he takes after Jenny, his mother.

It's not good, looking like somebody you've never met, because that means you can't work out what you're going to look like when you grow up. He pulls his hat still further down over his forehead, so that he can only see with one eye.

If we lived by the sea I'd be able to go down to the shore and look out for ships, he thinks.

A year ago, when he was ten, it was never difficult to go down to the river and pretend it was the sea. Now that he's eleven, that's only occasionally possible. It gets more and more difficult to imagine things.

He pulls his hat down over the other eye as well. Now he can only see out through the gaps between the threads. He's caught his face like a fish in a net.

He decides to go down to the riverbank and see if the snow has melted around his rock. He pulls his hat back up and breaks into a run.

He tries to think about why it's getting more and more difficult to imagine that the river is really the sea, but it's not easy to think when you're running.

He takes a short cut through Bodin's timber yard, and hears all the squeaking and whistling from the saws. Then he slides along the ice that always forms in the spring on the hill down towards the bakery. Once he's passed the bakery there's only the long slope down to the riverbank left. The snow is deep there, and he has to trudge through it. Once he's come that far, he suddenly finds it easier to use his imagination. It's not so difficult once all the buildings and people have been left behind.

The snow he is trudging through is a desert. Vultures are circling over his head, waiting for him to collapse with exhaustion and be unable to get up again. He's all alone in the desert, and in the far distance is his rock. If only he can struggle as far as that, he'll be able to survive . . .

Suddenly, he stops dead.

There's a boy he's never seen before sitting on his rock.

He's completely motionless, and he's looking through a telescope.

Joel crouches down in the snow.

This is the first time anybody has ever encroached on Joel's rock.

Who is he?

Joel is quite sure he's never set eyes on him before. He's a stranger, unknown.

Why is he sitting here by the river? What is he looking at through the telescope? Where has he come from?

Joel cowers down in the snow like a scared rabbit, not taking his eyes off the unknown boy for a moment.

There is a clattering noise from up on the bridge. The gates close and a goods train comes chugging along through the trees. The smoke from the engine's chimney puffs up into the sky, as if it's the trees that are breathing. The unknown boy aims his telescope at the train.

Joel can see that he's about his own age. Possibly slightly older. Instead of a woolly hat he's wearing a peaked cap with ear flaps.

But what has he got on his feet? They look like tennis rackets. Snowshoes!

The stranger is wearing snowshoes!

Joel has never seen any snowshoes before, only read about them in one of his father's books.

He presses himself down deeper into the snow, even though he's starting to feel cold.

Who is that boy sitting on his rock?

At that very moment the stranger turns round and looks straight at Joel.

'What are you lying there for?' he asks. 'Did you think I hadn't seen you?'

Joel couldn't think of anything sensible to say. He'd thought he was invisible, lying there in the snow. The boy on his rock has been looking through his telescope all the time, after all. How could he possibly have seen Joel?

The unknown boy jumps down from the rock and starts walking towards Joel on his snowshoes. Joel notes that what he has read in his father's books is true: when you are wearing snowshoes, your feet don't sink into the snow.

The boy stops in front of Joel.

'Are you thinking of staying there for good?' he says.

Joel still couldn't think of anything to say. Besides, the unknown boy is speaking with a peculiar accent. And he's smirking. Smirking non-stop.

'Who are you?' Joel asks eventually, standing up.

Although they are the same height, Joel looks like a dwarf, up to his knees in snow.

'I moved here today,' says the boy. 'I didn't want to, but I was forced to.'

Joel brushes himself down as he thinks.

'Where do you come from?' he asks.

'That doesn't matter,' the boy answers. 'I shan't be staying here anyway.'

Joel notices that the boy with the snowshoes is red-eyed, as if he'd been crying.

Joel suddenly loses control over himself. He says something he hadn't intended to say at all.

When he hears the words spurting out of his mouth, he regrets them right away: but it's too late by then.

'Those of us who live here don't sit down by the river and start blubbering,' he says.

The unknown boy looks at him in surprise. Joel wonders if he might be about to get beaten up. The boy in the snowshoes looks strong.

'I haven't been sitting here crying,' says the boy. 'I rubbed my face with my glove. I forgot that I am allergic to wool. That's why my eyes are red.'

Joel thinks he understands. There is a girl in his class who starts sneezing whenever anybody smelling of dog comes into the room. It must be the same thing.

'My name's Ture,' says the boy with the snowshoes.

Then he walks off, as if he's not the slightest bit interested in knowing that Joel is called Joel.

Joel watches him go, walking straggle-legged over the snow.

Whoever he is, he can keep away from my rock, he thinks. If he comes back here again I shall have to think up some way of scaring him off.

He trudges up the slope, stepping in his old footprints.

Snowshoes and a telescope, he thinks. Who is he?

*   *   *

The next day Joel looks round to see if there is anybody new in the school, but he can only see the familiar faces in the playground. As soon as lessons have finished Joel hurries down to the river again.

As soon as he passes the bakery he can see somebody sitting on the rock in the distance.

Once again he trudges down the slope, cursing inwardly because he doesn't have any snowshoes.

72

'I thought it was you,' said the unknown boy as Joel comes wading up through the snow.

'That's my rock,' says Joel, and he can feel his voice shaking with anger. 'Nobody else is allowed to sit on it, only me.'

'Do you have a title deed?' asks the unknown boy, with a grin.

Title deed? What's that? wonders Joel.

'If you own a rock you have to have a title deed,' says the boy. 'A certificate of ownership, with an official stamp. You have to have that.'

'It's my rock,' says Joel angrily.

His voice isn't shaking any more. He's just angry now.

The boy suddenly jumps down from the rock and Joel feels sure there's going to be a fight. If the rock is his, he will have to defend it. But instead the boy undoes the straps fastening the snowshoes to his boots.

'Would you like to try them?' he says.

Joel looks at him. Is he being serious?

'That rock is mine,' he says again.

'I've no intention of taking it off you,' says the boy. 'Are you going to try the snowshoes or aren't you?'

Joel fastens the straps round his boots.

It's a remarkable feeling, being able to walk on the snow. It makes him twice as tall. If I have a pair of snowshoes on, I'm as big as a grown-up, he thinks.

'They were very good,' he says as he returns them. 'They really were very good.'

'What else are you called, besides Joel?' the unknown boy suddenly asks.

How on earth does the stranger know that he's called Joel?

'Gustafson,' he replies. 'But how do you know my name's Joel?'

'It's carved into the rock,' says the boy. 'It must be you if you say the rock belongs to you.'

Joel had forgotten that. Scratching his name into the rock last autumn, with a rusty old nail.

'What about you?' he asks. 'Apart from Ture?'

'Swallow. But I'm a nobleman and so

I'm called von Swallow. Ture von Swallow.'

'Eh?' says Joel. 'Surely nobody can have a name like that? And why don't you go to school? Why have you moved here? Where the hell do you live?'

'My dad's the new district judge,' says Ture. 'We live over the courthouse. I don't need to go to school because it's in the middle of term. Dad fixed that. I'm working at home. But I start school in the autumn. Or so they think. I'll have run away by then. It's not possible to live here. So I shall run away.'

He takes off one of his gloves and checks his watch.

'In one week, three days, seven hours and nine minutes from now I shall run away,' he says. 'Just in case you're interested.'

Joel gapes at him.

Not that he has his mouth wide open. It's an invisible mouth inside him that's gaping.

He's never heard a lie like that before. First the boy with the

75

snowshoes claims that he's a nobleman and is called Swallow. Then he says he's going to run away and gives the exact time. Joel would never be able to think up a lie like that. The boy with the snowshoes must be somebody pretty special.

'Why?' he asks. 'Why are you going to run away just then?'

'Because there's a train leaving for Orsa at that time,' says the boy with the snowshoes. 'Because Dad will be busy with the sessions then. Nobody will notice me carrying out my suitcase. There's a lot of stuff I need to take with me. That's why it's important that nobody sees me. I could really do with somebody to help me carry it. Maybe you could do that?'

'Of course I could,' says Joel. 'I've thought about running away as well.'

What a lie, Joel thinks. He lies so convincingly that it almost seems true.

'Show me something exciting,' says the boy. 'If there is anything exciting to show round here.'

Joel trudges after Ture, who is taking big strides on top of the snow.

Perhaps he'll give me his snowshoes if I help him to run away, Joel thinks.

That's not true, of course. But still...

They get as far as the bakery, and it's starting to get dark already.

Out of the blue, Joel knows what he is going to do.

'There is a secret,' he says. 'But it's at night. Only at night. Maybe you'll be asleep then?'

'I'll be there,' says Ture.

Joel thinks.

Opposite the courthouse are the marshalling yards. There are always goods wagons waiting to be connected to some train or other the next day.

'I'll be waiting for you next to the goods wagons,' he says. 'At midnight. But I shan't wait long.'

'What happens at night?' asks Ture.

'It's not sure that anything will happen at all,' says Joel. 'But there's a secret society.'

'I'll be there,' says Ture. 'My room is in the attic, but I can set up a ladder.'

Joel is in a hurry now. The potatoes ought to have been boiling on the

77

stove already. Samuel will soon be home. And he has to prepare for tonight as well. Being the only member of a Secret Society is one thing. Not being alone any more will be something completely different.

'See you, then,' he says. 'I have to go home now.'

'Where do you live?' asks Ture.

'You'll find out tonight,' says Joel.

It's only when he's bounding up the stairs that he remembers he was supposed to collect a kilo of coffee from the shop.

He unlocks the door and before he's even taken off his boots he checks to see how much coffee is left in the tin on the shelf over the stove. Enough for one more day, so he can breathe again. His dad would have gone through the roof if they'd run out of coffee.

He can go and get the coffee himself, Joel thinks, as he sits down on the cold floor in the dark entrance hall. I haven't got time. Being responsible for a Secret Society means that you only seldom have time to boil potatoes.

Joel curses the kindling in the stove

that refuses to light. He runs through all the swearwords he knows, forwards and backwards, but still he can't make the wood catch fire. He starts running through his range of swearwords once again, at top volume; but he calms down when old Mrs Westman starts bashing on her ceiling with her walking stick.

At last it starts burning. Joel gives the potatoes a quick scrub, and pours some water and a pinch of salt into the big pan. Four big potatoes for Dad, three little ones for himself.

Then he goes to the showcase and carefully lifts up *Celestine* and takes out his logbook. Samuel might turn up at any moment, so he doesn't have much time before the heavy footsteps start echoing up the stairs.

He's caught on to the fact that it's easier to think when he writes. And there's an awful lot of things he needs to make up his mind about.

Just what should he tell Ture?

The Secret Society hasn't exactly done very much. Can he really admit that he's the only member? He thinks about what Ture has said, about what's going to happen in a week's time.

Joel has never seriously thought about running away. You have to know where you're going to when you run away. You have to have a plan, some special aim in mind.

If he knew the whereabouts of his mum, Jenny, he could have set out to discover what she looked like.

If he'd had a telescope like Ture, he could have hidden behind a bush and spied on her. No doubt she is so like him that it would be like examining yourself in a mirror.

Children do not take after their parents, he decides, as he puts another piece of firewood into the stove. It's the parents who take after their children.

The only times he's thought of running away have been when he's been angry with his father. That time when he was given a stool instead of a kite, he thought about wandering off into the forest and lying down in the snow to die. His dad would find him the next morning when he set out into the forest to work.

He listens for footsteps on the stairs, then sits down at the kitchen table again. I'll have to use my imagination, he thinks. I'll have to make up whatever doesn't exist for real.

If Ture is going to run away next week, he'll never find out that what Joel tells him isn't true.

He writes down the names of his classmates that he likes: they can become members of The Secret Society. The ones he doesn't like, such as Otto, will be excluded. They have committed serious acts of treachery and been forced out of the society.

He also writes down the name on the grave he generally jumps over in the cemetery. Nils Wiberg is a member of the society who died in mysterious circumstances. Then he remembers Rev. Sundin, the old dean, who died last year, the day after the end of term. He can also be a member who died in unusual circumstances. And the judge who died on the steps outside Stora Hotellet! What was his name? Törnqvist? He can also be a dead member.

He suddenly recalls what Ture had said. About living over the courthouse, and his dad being a district judge. That means he must be the replacement for Törnqvist, he decides. Now I have something I can show Ture. The icy step he slipped on and broke his neck.

That was as far as he got, as the front door banged and he could hear footsteps approaching up the stairs.

He listens to the stamping of his father's feet. What do they sound like today?

It's quite loud, but he doesn't sound angry or weary. They're not bottle-steps today, more like storytelling-steps. Real seafarer's strides.

Even so, there's something not quite right about them. There seems to be a sort of echo.

Joel hurriedly replaces the logbook under *Celestine* and sticks a fork into the biggest of the potatoes.

The flat door opens and Joel understands why the footsteps sounded so odd.

His father is not alone.

Behind him is a woman in a red hat, black overcoat and rubber overshoes. Joel recognises her immediately. It's Sara, who works as a waitress in the local bar. Big-breasted Sara, who wanders around balancing trays and beer bottles and is always laughing so that you can see the big gap in her bottom teeth.

That slut! What's she doing here?

Joel has occasionally been in the bar to sell copies of the local weekly paper. He's watched Sara weaving her way among the tables carrying bottles and a rag. If anybody gets drunk or tries to grope her breasts, she shouts for the ill-tempered bouncer Ek, who's always fluttering around like a bat outside the Gents. Between them they eject the drunkard or the groper. Joel has seen such goings-on as he's moved from table to table, trying to sell newspapers.

He doesn't know what her surname is. But he doesn't like her. Her breasts are too big and she smells of perfume, beer and sweat. There have actually been occasions when he's thought it's a good job she isn't his mother.

But here she is now, standing in the hall and laughing just as loud as she does in the bar.

Why is she here? Joel asks himself uneasily. Why is she hanging up her overcoat and taking off her overshoes? And why is she still wearing that red hat?

They come into the kitchen and Joel notices straight away that his father smells of beer. Beer and sweat and wet wool.

But he's not drunk. He isn't swaying and his eyes are not red. But his hair is standing on end, and Joel doesn't like it when his father looks like that.

That slut Sara is still wearing her waitress outfit, he sees. White blouse with a beer stain in the middle of one of her enormous breasts. Black skirt with a little hole in one of the seams.

Joel is getting more and more worried.

This is the first time his father has ever brought somebody back home after a day working in the forest.

Joel has always thought that his dad's

84

friends are sailors plying the various oceans. Friends who are waiting for him to drop that axe, pack his sailor's chest standing in the hall, and set out once more for the endless seas.

How could he bring this slut back home with him?

'Sara's come back with me for a cup of coffee,' says Samuel, patting Joel on the shoulder.

'There isn't any coffee,' says Joel quick as a flash.

'What do you mean by that?' Samuel asks. He's smiling all the time.

'We've run out,' says Joel. 'I didn't have time to go to the shop. There's enough for you tomorrow morning. But not for her.'

'Never mind,' says Sara with a laugh. She pats his cheek.

That's when Joel decides he is going to kill her. It will be the next mission for The Secret Society, once they've found the dog that headed for a star.

'So you are Joel, then,' she says. 'Haven't I seen you in the bar now and then, selling newspapers?'

Joel doesn't answer.

Samuel shakes the coffee tin. Strangely enough he doesn't seem to be angry. He ought to be. Inviting somebody back for coffee only to find that Joel has forgotten to call at the shop as usual.

Can that slut in the red hat really put him in such a good mood?

He suddenly has an awful thought.

Perhaps his father is going to remarry! In which case Joel would risk having brothers and sisters with Sara as their mother . . .

No, that can't be possible. A sailor can't marry a waitress in a bar.

'A lovely place you've got here,' she says, wandering round the kitchen and having a good look.

'It's annoying that we don't have any coffee,' says Samuel, giving Joel a dirty look.

'Oh, it doesn't matter,' she says. Then she pats Joel on the cheek again. Her hand is big and red and rough.

'How did it go at school today?' she asks.

Joel mumbles something inaudible in reply.

'You're a real misery today, aren't you?' says Samuel, sitting down on the sofa.

That's a betrayal. Joel is petrified. Whose side is he on? Is he putting on a show for Sara and her red hat? Is he letting his own son down?

Sara sits down on Joel's chair and straightens out a fold in the tablecloth with her big hand.

'You can invite me to coffee another time, Samuel,' she says.

So she intends coming round again, then? If she does I shall run away, Joel thinks. Samuel can sit here on his own, gaping at her red hat.

'I'm going to my room,' says Joel.

He closes the door, goes down on one knee and peers out at the kitchen through the keyhole.

He's afraid his father is about to disappear. Sara with the red hat has started to eat him up.

When she speaks he nods and smiles and seems extremely interested.

What are they talking about? A new grocer's shop that's due to open shortly. Why is he interested in that?

87

He's never the one who goes shopping!

Plums. Prunes. Good for constipation.

Why is he pretending to be interested in that?

Nearly half an hour later he kneels down again and looks through the keyhole. His knees and back are aching, but he has to keep an eye on his father.

I'll kill her, he thinks. If I don't, she'll take my dad away from me.

In the end she gets to her feet.

Joel can hardly straighten his stiff knees and barely has time to dash over to his bed, lie down and pretend to be reading a book.

Samuel opens the door.

'Sara's leaving now,' he says. 'Come and say goodbye.'

I don't want to, he thinks. But of course, he does go out into the kitchen.

' 'Bye, 'bye, Joel,' she says as she buttons up her coat. 'The next time you come to the bar, I'll make sure the customers buy all your newspapers.'

Then they're alone, Joel and his dad.

'Did you hear that?' asks Samuel.

'Go there and sell lots of newspapers and earn a bit of pocket money.'

Joel lays the table while his father fries some pork. He clatters away with the pan, humming an old sea shanty.

While they are eating Joel decides to get his own back. He can see that his dad is thinking about Sara all the time. He must get him to think about something else.

'I want a bike,' he says. 'I'm the only one who doesn't have a bike.'

But his father doesn't hear him. Sara with the red hat has started eating up his thoughts.

'A bike,' he says, louder this time.

Samuel turns to look at him.

'I beg your pardon?'

'I want a bike. I don't want to be the only one who doesn't have a bike.'

'Of course you shall have a bicycle,' says his father. 'I've already been thinking about that. The next time I collect my wages we shall go and buy you a bicycle.'

Is that really true? wonders Joel. Has he really thought about it of his own accord?

Suddenly there's so much that Joel doesn't understand.

Is this what it's like to be grown up? Doing and saying things that children don't understand?

'It was fun to have a visitor,' says Samuel. 'Usually it's just you and me, sitting gaping at each other.'

'Are you going to get married again?' asks Joel.

'No,' says his father. 'I haven't got round to thinking about that. But it does get lonely sometimes.'

'Tell me about my mum,' says Joel.

Samuel puts down his fork and gives him a serious look.

'Soon,' he says. 'But not just now. Not when I'm in such a good mood . . .'

When they've finished eating Joel builds a little cabin in his bed. His blanket and the bedcover over two chairs make an excellent hiding place. He creeps inside it and starts thinking.

Far too much has happened at the same time.

First of all the boy with the snowshoes turns up. And they'll be going out together tonight. Then Sara comes visiting. And next his dad says that of course Joel can have a bike.

That's too much.

Thoughts are buzzing around inside his head and Joel has trouble in pinning them down. He knows you have to take one thing at a time, but that's easier said than done just now. What he would most like to do is to go to sleep and dream about The Flying Horse. But he hasn't time for that. He has to make preparations for the night. He has to be absolutely clear about all the things he's going to make up so that Ture doesn't start suspecting anything. But it's not easy to concentrate because Sara keeps intruding on his thoughts in her overshoes and her red hat, and with the big hand she keeps using to pat him on the cheek.

The cabin doesn't help. He just feels impatient.

He goes into his father's room: Samuel is sitting in his chair with his eyes closed, listening to the radio.

Joel does something most unusual.

He sits on his father's knee.

'Phew, you're as heavy as a tree trunk,' gasps his dad. 'You're crushing the life out of me.'

On the radio some nasty-sounding voice is bleating on about a journey with a motorbike and sidecar through Italy.

'Genoa,' says Samuel out of the blue. 'I've been there.'

'But I haven't,' says Joel. 'Not yet, at least.'

Samuel chuckles so violently that his stomach bounces up and down. But he doesn't explain why he's laughing.

The sidecar trip comes to an end and is followed by some marching music. Samuel beats time with one foot. But soon he hasn't the strength to keep Joel on his knee any longer.

'You're too heavy,' he says. 'I don't understand how you can be so thin and yet weigh so much.'

Then he turns serious.

'Sara,' he says. 'The lady who was here. She had a boy just like you once. But he died in a fire. Him and his dad. They were living a long way from here

92

at the time. She moved here after that. It must be hard to be reminded of it all every time she sees somebody like you.'

When Joel has gone to bed and his dad has sat with him for a while and tucked him in, he thinks about that fire.

As long as Sara doesn't eat up his dad, she's welcome to come round for coffee some time.

As long as she doesn't take his dad away from him . . .

He lies in the dark and has trouble in staying awake. Several hours to go yet before midnight, a lot of waiting to do.

He would really have preferred it to be another evening. It's never good to have too much to think about at the same time. Even so, he eventually hears his dad gargling in the kitchen, and then everything goes quiet.

He lies in bed watching the luminous hands on his alarm clock. They are moving incredibly slowly towards midnight. At a quarter to twelve he tiptoes out through the door. He thinks the hall still smells of Sara.

It's a calm, starry night. Maybe Ture won't turn up, he thinks. Even so, he hurries along the deserted streets and stands in the shadow of a goods wagon in the marshalling yard.

The white courthouse with its columned balcony is in darkness. There's no sign of any light at all.

Joel waits . . .

5

In the far distance Joel can see the yellow clockface in the church tower. If he screws his eyes up, he can just make out the two hands. Five minutes past midnight.

He stamps his feet to keep warm.

The goods wagon beside him is big and dark, like a dinosaur chained up in its cage.

He imagines a goods wagon being able to think. What would happen if a goods wagon started growling? Who will go hunting for a goods wagon if it breaks away from its chains and escapes?

'Only people can think,' he whispers to himself. 'Only people . . .'

He suddenly gives a start.

He has the feeling somebody out there in the darkness is looking at him. He turns round quickly, but sees nothing apart from the silent goods wagons.

He gazes over towards the district court, but everything is dark and quiet. No lights in any of the black windows.

He starts to feel scared. Somebody is watching him in the darkness. He's quite sure of it, even though he can't see nor hear anything.

He holds his breath and listens.

Somebody is breathing close by.

He listens again, but thinks he is imagining it.

Then he feels a hand on his shoulder.

Death, he thinks. It must be death. An iron talon digging into his shoulder . . .

He screams into the darkness.

'Did I scare you?' asks Ture, who is standing behind him.

When he sees that it's Ture, it

registers that he very nearly peed himself. That would have been catastrophic. When you pee yourself and it's freezing cold outside, you first feel warm, but then it soon gets so cold that you can't stop shivering.

'I'm pretty good at creeping up on people,' says Ture. 'I've been watching you for several minutes. Who were you talking to? I heard you whispering.'

'To myself,' says Joel. 'Could you hear me?'

Ture nods.

Joel can't see properly, but he has the impression Ture is smirking.

Joel is beginning to feel unsure about his secret society. He doesn't know enough about Ture. What kind of thoughts does a person have when he says he's a nobleman and, in all seriousness, claims that his name is von Swallow? The only thing Joel is sure is good is the heroism rule he has invented.

Joel leads the way through the dark streets, down towards the iron bridge over the river. He takes short cuts through rear courtyards and narrow alleys between cold walls. Although it's not necessary, he picks the most roundabout and awkward route he can think of. Clambering over the roof of the shed where the Highways Department keeps its welding equipment is unnecessary, of course. Nor is it essential to struggle through the broken-down greenhouse owned by Mr Under, the horse dealer. But Ture doesn't complain. He follows a couple of paces behind Joel, and Joel notices that he's good at climbing.

They pause outside the block of flats where Otto lives.

'This is where an enemy lives,' says Joel. 'He's been excluded. He's called Otto and he's a real bastard.'

'Excluded from what?' wonders Ture.

The light from a streetlamp illuminates his face, and Joel can see that he is not grinning scornfully.

'You'll find out soon enough,' says Joel. 'How old are you, by the way?'

'Twelve,' says Ture. 'You as well?'

'Nearly,' says Joel.

When they stop the next time they're

in the middle of the railway bridge. The enormous arches tower up over their heads.

Joel quickly invents another rule. Too bad if it's a rule that is going to cause pain.

He bends down and touches the ice-cold parapet with his tongue. His tongue sticks to the metal immediately, and it hurts when he pulls it loose.

Then Joel tells Ture about The Secret Society. About who is in it, who has been excluded and who are dead. He talks about the dog he is looking for, but he doesn't mention that he imagines it is on its way to a star. He's not sure why he keeps that back. Perhaps he wants to keep some of the secret for himself?

'Even if you're going to run away in a week's time you can still be a member,' says Joel. 'But there's something you must promise, and another thing you must do. You must hold your tongue against the bridge parapet and count up to fifty. And you must promise to crawl over those enormous iron arches if you betray The Secret Society.'

Without hesitation Ture crouches down and presses his tongue against the freezing cold parapet.

Joel realises straight away that Ture has never done this before. Licked cold iron in the middle of winter. The trick is simply to touch the iron with the very tip of your tongue, so that it doesn't hurt too much when you try to take it away.

Joel is worried. What if he can't get it loose again? What if it sticks fast and is torn off?

When Ture has finished counting to fifty he pulls his tongue away. Joel can see that it hurts something awful, and that Ture wasn't prepared for that at all. He pulls a face and spits blood into the palm of his hand.

'I promise,' he says. 'I'll crawl over the arch if I betray The Secret Society.'

'You have to stand up at the top of the arch and pee into the river as well,' says Joel.

'I have no intention of evading my obligations,' says Ture. 'Now what do we do?'

'Look for the dog,' says Joel.

But there is no sign of the dog that night.

They roam about the little town.

The Old Bricklayer, Simon Windstorm, goes past in his lorry, and Joel explains that the driver is a madman who never sleeps.

'He hasn't slept for thirty-four years,' he says, to make Simon even more mysterious.

'You'll die,' says Ture. 'If you haven't slept for as many years as that, you're dead. That would mean there's a dead man driving around in that lorry.'

'Maybe he is dead,' says Joel. 'We'll look into that one of these nights.'

Outside the Grand Hotel are a couple of drunks, leaning against each other. Joel recognises them. The short fat one is Mr Rudin, the ironmonger. The tall thin one is Walter Kringström who runs a dance orchestra and plays the clarinet.

In the background, in the forecourt of the hotel, Mr Roth, the restaurant owner, is trying to start his car. He can't get the engine to fire, and they hear Roth cursing and swearing as he rummages around under the bonnet.

Rudin and Kringström make their way unsteadily as far as the furniture shop where they come to a halt again, leaning on each other. Joel thinks it looks as if Walter Kringström is crying and the ironmonger is trying to console him.

'Winos,' hisses Ture in his ear. 'Let's get going . . .'

They wander through the empty streets for another hour. Occasionally The Old Bricklayer drives past in his lorry.

Joel is afraid that Ture might get bored. I ought to have hit upon more things to do, he thinks. If only Samuel hadn't come home with that slut in the red hat in tow . . .

He thinks he knows where she lives, behind the bookshop, in an attic flat.

He carefully opens the gate leading into the rear courtyard.

'Another enemy lives here,' he informs Ture in a low voice. 'The Lady in the Red Hat. She should be eliminated.'

'Why?' asks Ture. 'Who is she?'

'She serves beer in the local bar,' says Joel. 'She's broken into my flat.'

'Why don't you go to the police?' wonders Ture.

'Not that kind of break-in,' says Joel.

Then he remembers that he's promised to show Ture where he lives.

He's not sure he still wants to, in fact.

What is a shabby old wooden house in need of a coat of paint compared with the district courthouse? He might just as well show Ture the broken-down shed behind the vicarage. Or the earth cellar in the yard behind the pharmacy.

But he acknowledges that he can't get out of it now, and he leads the way back down to the river.

He stops by the gate.

'This is where I live,' he says.

Ture gives the house a long, hard look.

'The whole house?' he asks.

Joel very nearly says yes, but that would have been a dangerous lie. A bad lie that could easily be disproved. It would have been a hopeless piece of boasting.

'Just the top floor,' he says.

Then their nocturnal expedition seems to grind to a halt of its own accord. They go back to the courthouse and say goodbye at the gate.

'I wish it was me,' says Joel. 'Not having to go to school, I mean.'

'Come here after school tomorrow,' says Ture. 'Ring the bell on that door over there, the middle one.' Then he jumps over the gate.

'It squeaks,' he says. 'The caretaker might wake up and think we're burglars.'

Then he spits into the palm of his hand and examines it.

'It's stopped bleeding,' he says. 'Will you be coming tomorrow?'

Joel nods. He stays by the gate and watches Ture disappear into the white house. Then he hurries home. He's so tired, he can hardly keep his eyes open. When The Old Bricklayer comes rattling past in his lorry he doesn't even bother to slink into the shadows. He'd like to know what Ture is

103

thinking. There's something about Ture that makes him insecure . . .

*   *   *

When Joel tiptoes carefully into the kitchen he can sense straight away that something is amiss. He stands perfectly still, listening.

When his eyes get used to the dark, he looks round the kitchen. Nothing has changed. *Celestine* is in her showcase, his dad's socks are hanging up to dry over the stove, which is still hot. Even so, something is not as it should be.

It's just that I'm tired, he thinks. I'm imagining things . . .

He takes off his boots, dries the wet stains from the floor, and snuggles into bed.

Although he has so much to think about, he falls asleep immediately.

Next day he hesitates for ages at the gate to the courthouse.

Should he go in, or shouldn't he? Had Ture been serious? The house is too big and too posh. He vaguely recalls hearing that the judge's lodgings has eleven rooms. Old Törnqvist used to live there all on his own. In eleven rooms?

In the end he plucks up courage and opens the gate. It squeaks, just as Ture had said. He walks down the stone path and rings the doorbell. Better take my cap off, he thinks, and removes his woolly hat. Ture answers the door, to his relief.

It could have been his mother. Or even worse, his father.

What on earth do you say to a district judge? You might get hard labour if you say something wrong.

The flat is just as big as Joel had imagined. He follows Ture through the many rooms in his stocking feet. The walls are full of big paintings in gilt frames, and the walls of one room are covered from top to bottom with books. There are thick carpets on all the floors, and a coat of armour stands in one corner. Joel stops to stare.

Fancy a coat of armour ending up in this remote, snow-filled dump.

'The armour is from Scotland,' says

Ture. 'That's where our ancestors come from.'

He and Ture seem to be the only ones in the enormous flat.

'Don't you have a mother?' asks Joel?

'Of course I have a mother,' says Ture. 'But she and my two sisters aren't moving here until the summer. It's just Dad and me at the moment. Plus somebody who comes in to clean and do the cooking. She's out shopping just now.'

Of course I have a mother—Joel repeats it to himself. It's not always of course . . .

Ture has a large room under the roof. Joel thinks it's odd that he's unpacked all his things and arranged them so neatly if he's going to run away shortly. And is he really going to cart all this with him when he does leave? He would need The Old Bricklayer's lorry to carry everything as far as the station.

For Joel, going into Ture's room is like entering a hitherto unknown world. It's almost as big as all the rooms in the flat Joel shares with his father put together. One wall is covered in books, another one in maps. Big model aeroplanes are suspended from the ceiling. Standing on a long table stretching from one corner to the other are Meccano models: steam engines and strange machines, the likes of which Joel has never seen before. There are two radios by the bed, and earphones hanging from some kind of pulley arrangement over the pillow. This room contains everything apart from toys.

Joel stands in the middle of the room, gaping at it all.

'You have a hole in your sock,' says Ture. 'Mind your big toe doesn't run away.'

'I like to keep my toes well aired,' says Joel.

He says it as nonchalantly as he can. He doesn't want to give the impression that he's embarrassed.

There is a picture hanging over the bed. It depicts a man with a long beard and an almost bald head. Joel thinks it looks like one of those old priests that are hanging in the sacristy at church.

'Who's that?' he asks, but regrets it the moment he's said it. Perhaps it's somebody he ought to recognise?

'Leonardo,' says Ture. 'The one and only Leonardo da Vinci. He's my idol.' Joel has never heard of him. Now he takes a big risk. If Ture starts asking questions, he'll be rumbled.

'Everybody knows who he is,' he says, as convincingly as he can. He's got away with it. Ture doesn't ask any more questions, but starts showing him his maps.

'I ought to have been born in another age,' he says. 'When there were still mountains and rivers and deserts to discover. No matter where you go nowadays, there's always somebody who's been there before you. I'm living too late.'

'You live when you live,' says Joel.

'Do you never dream?' asks Ture.

'No,' says Joel. 'Not very often.'

'You're lying,' says Ture.

'Oh no I'm not,' says Joel.

'I have my own ideas about that,' says

Ture. 'But what do you want to be when you grow up?'

'A sailor, I think,' says Joel. 'Like my dad.'

'But there can't be any sailors living round here, surely?' says Ture. 'There's no sea.'

'He lives here even so,' says Joel.

'Is he a captain?' asks Ture.

Joel would prefer not to answer. If he does, he'll have to lie even more. He doesn't want to say that his dad is only an Able Seaman.

'His last voyage was as captain on a boat called *Celestine*,' he says. 'They were transporting live horses.'

He suddenly feels angry with his father. Why isn't he a captain? Then they could have lived in a big house, like this one.

'I might become an engineer,' says Ture. 'Or maybe I'll work for the UN.'

Joel has only a vague idea of what the UN is. A sort of place where people give speeches for the rest to listen to. But he doesn't ask.

I can go to the library and look them up, he thinks. Leonardo da Vinci and the UN.

'Why do you have two radio sets?' he asks, so as to avoid having to talk about the UN.

'So that I can listen to two programmes at the same time,' says Ture. 'Sweden and foreign stations at the same time.'

Once again Joel is angry with his dad. Here we have a boy aged twelve with two radio sets. His dad is over forty, but he has only one. And that's much older than the two Ture has.

'What kind of a radio do you have?' asks Ture.

'A Luxor,' says Joel.

Ture sits on the floor, on a cushion. 'The Secret Society is good,' says Ture. 'But we could do more than just look for a dog.'

'But you're going to run away soon,' says Joel. 'I thought we could find that dog while you're still here.'

'A Secret Society must create fear,' says Ture. 'We have to show that we're dangerous.'

'How?' asks Joel.

'I can show you tonight,' says Ture.

In fact Joel had intended staying at home tonight. He's frightened of falling asleep at his desk if he goes out every night. But he doesn't say that.

They agree to meet at midnight, among the goods wagons. Then Joel has to leave. The stove and potatoes are waiting for him.

'Why are you in such a hurry?' asks Ture.

'That's a secret,' says Joel.

He's in a bad mood when he goes home. He has too many lies to keep track of. And it's all his dad's fault. He's not a captain, he has only one radio set, and he hasn't got a wife which means that Joel hasn't got a mum.

Samuel has nothing. Only an axe that he uses to cut down trees in the forest.

Even worse, he's never said anything about who Leonardo da Vinci is, or what they do at the UN.

And to top it all he comes home with that slut in the red hat in tow.

Joel remembers that he has to go to the shop. As he's nearly home, he has to retrace his steps. That makes him even angrier.

I'm going to move in with Jenny, my mum, he thinks. I don't care what she looks like, I don't care what she does. Nothing can be worse than living with Samuel. The only thing he'll take with him is *Celestine*.

He'll take that blue stool he got for his birthday to the railway bridge and hurl it into the river.

There's a queue in the shop. Svenson smells of strong drink as usual, fumbles with the goods and has trouble in working out the bills. Joel waits and waits.

It will never be his turn. That's his dad's fault as well.

When Joel gets home he starts the fire in the stove, then lies down on the kitchen bench while he's waiting for the potatoes to boil. He falls asleep, and is woken up by his father shaking him by the shoulder.

The meal is ready and the table set. Samuel is in an extremely good mood. He's humming one of his sea shanties. He keeps smiling at Joel.

After dinner he gets shaved. That's

enough to worry Joel. His dad only ever gets shaved once a week, on Saturday afternoons. It's only Wednesday today. Samuel is humming away non-stop.

Joel decides he'll have to keep a close eye on his father.

Can Sara with the red hat really put him in such a good mood? Or is it something else?

After dinner Joel takes out his thirteen tin soldiers and builds a fort out of some books. But he finds it hard to concentrate because he can hear his dad humming away in his room all the time.

In the end he gives his model soldiers a kick and they all end up under the bed.

They can stay there until they're buried in dust, he thinks.

Then he goes into his father's room. Samuel is lying on his bed, listening to the radio and wiggling his toes.

'Hi, Joel,' he says. 'What are you playing with?'

'I'm not playing,' says Joel. 'I want to know who Leonardo da Vinci is.'

'Who?'

'Leonardo da Vinci.'

'That's a name I've heard before. Why do you want to know who he is?'

'I just do.'

'Hang on, I'll have to think a bit. Leonardo da Vinci . . .'

Joel stands in the doorway, waiting. His dad wiggles his toes and thinks.

'He was an inventor, I think. And a painter. A long time ago. He knew everything. He invented cannons and aeroplanes long before anybody else.'

'I'm going to be like him.'

'Nobody can be like him. You can only be who you are.'

'Why did you never become a captain?'

'I didn't have any schooling. I just had my hands. That means you can only be an Able Seaman.'

Joel thinks he ought to tell him to stop wiggling his toes. Stop smiling, stop humming sea shanties. But he just stands in the doorway and says nothing.

'I'll go back to my room, then,' he says.

His father doesn't answer. He's closed his eyes and is humming a tune.

If he's lying there thinking of Sara, I'm off, Joel thinks. If he brings her home one more time, I'm getting out of here.

He will need to find out where his mother lives. He'll have to ask his dad about that. It's the most important of all the questions currently occupying his mind. He wishes it was the only thing he had to worry about. Most of the time nothing at all happens, he thinks, but just now far too much is happening that he needs to think through. It gets more difficult to cope with life for every year that passes, he thinks. Not the least difficult thing is understanding grown-ups, understanding his father.

He wishes he could creep into Samuel's head and sit down in the middle of all his thoughts. Then he would be able to compare what his dad says with what he actually thinks.

Perhaps being a grown-up means not saying what you really think.

Or knowing which lies are least

dangerous. Learning to avoid untruths that can too easily be found out . . .

He takes his alarm clock into bed with him and wraps it inside a sock before placing it under his pillow, next to his ear. Then he switches off the light.

When Samuel sees that, he won't come in and sit on the edge of Joel's bed. He'll simply close the door and go to his own room.

It's easy to fool grown-ups, he thinks. Just because you've switched the light off, they think you're asleep.

What he would really like, in fact, is for his father to come and sit on his bed even so. Sit down and tell him about Jenny without Joel having to ask first.

It's hard to settle down to sleep. The alarm clock is rubbing against his ear. He shudders at the thought of having to get dressed in a few hours' time and go out into the night. He wonders what it is that Ture is going to show him.

Create fear, he said. What does he mean by that?

Joel tosses and turns. The alarm

116

clock is irritating him, and he has to check and make sure he hasn't accidentally switched it off.

He needs to do a lot of thinking about Ture.

Having met him is both a good thing and a bad thing. Good that he's going to run away in a week's time because Joel has said various things that can be found out as untrue. But at the same time, it's a bad thing that he will no longer be around. It's good having a nobleman as a friend. A nobleman who is older than Joel.

He thinks about the enormous flat. He pictures himself in all the different rooms. Looking at the paintings and books, walking on the soft carpets.

But when he comes to the suit of armour, he stops dead.

Now he's on his own, Ture is no longer in his thoughts, and he can put on the armour with no risk of being found out. Last of all he closes the visor.

Now he's on a battlefield somewhere.

Miss Nederström has told them that it was always misty when knights in armour rode into battle.

Now he's mounting his steed, the magnificent stallion he's seen at Mr Under's, the horse dealer. The black horse with the white patch under his right eye. Somewhere in the distance, invisible in the mist, the enemy is waiting . . .

He gives a start when Samuel opens the door.

It takes a long time to build up a good dream, but all it needs is for his dad to take hold of the door handle, and it's all gone.

He pretends to be asleep.

Samuel closes the door gently.

He usually listens for longer than that, Joel thinks. Tonight it happened far too quickly. As if he were hoping that I'd be asleep.

There ought to be rules for fathers, thinks Joel angrily. They shouldn't be allowed to come bursting into a dream. They should only be allowed to listen so long at the door to see if you're asleep. They shouldn't be allowed to invite certain people home for coffee.

All fathers ought to be made to sign

such rules. And every time they break one, they should be punished.

The radio falls silent, Samuel has a good gargle, and his bed creaks.

What actually happened? Joel wonders.

Why was Jenny so unhappy? What happened?

When the alarm starts buzzing under his pillow, he's not sure at first what it is. It goes off when he's in the middle of a dream. Joel is surrounded by strangers, but he knows that his mother is among them somewhere. The only person he recognises is The Old Bricklayer. Then the barriers at the level crossing start ringing. It's the alarm clock under his pillow.

He lies still in the darkness, listening.

What had he been dreaming about? Was it a nasty dream? Or just an odd one?

He keeps on listening. Silence always has many sounds.

A beam creaks. He hears his own breathing. There's a rushing sound in his ears, like the wind.

Joel is afraid of the dark. Not being

able to see the walls and ceiling, not being able to see his own hands. Waking up in the dark is a kind of loneliness he's scared of.

It's the nearest he can imagine to death.

A black room where the ceiling could be just above his face, but he can't see it.

When you wake up in the middle of the night there's no way of knowing if you're the only person left in the whole wide world.

He switches on the lamp standing on the blue stool. Then he switches it off again. The darkness isn't frightening any more. Not now that he knows nothing has changed while he's been asleep.

He tiptoes into the kitchen, puts on his boots then creeps silently down the stairs. Old Mrs Westman is having a coughing fit.

The stars are twinkling in a clear sky when he gets outside, and he starts running so as not to be late. Ture is waiting for him by the goods wagons, in the shadows. Once again he creeps up on Joel from behind and grabs him by the shoulder, making him jump.

I ought to have known, thinks Joel. Ture will keep on doing that for as long as he sees it makes me jump.

First they go looking for the dog. Joel shows Ture the streetlight where he last saw the dog. He'd like to tell the story of the night when he carried The Flying Horse out of the bicycle shop— but would Ture believe him? Joel has no idea what Ture thinks. And when he runs away next week it will be too late. After that he'll never get to know anything.

It strikes Joel that this is the first time he's met anybody who he knows he's soon going to be separated from, and will never see again. Never ever, as long as he lives . . .

'A dog,' says Ture without warning. 'Why are we looking for a dog?'

Joel doesn't know what to say. All he knows is that the dog is important. The dog heading for a star.

He can't explain it, he just knows . . .

Ture suddenly pokes him in the back. 'There's somebody coming,' he

121

whispers.

He points down the street, and Joel sees a figure in dark clothes approaching along the opposite pavement. Somebody lit up by a streetlamp before being swallowed up by the darkness again.

They stand next to the wall where they are sure of not being seen. The darkly clad figure has its head bowed, looking like a body that stops at the shoulders. But Joel sees who it is.

It's No-Nose. The woman with a handkerchief instead of a nose in her face.

'It's Gertrud,' he whispers into Ture's ear. 'I know who she is.'

'Why is she out in the middle of the night, walking with her head bowed?' wonders Ture.

Ture indicates that they should follow her. They sneak along in the shadow of the house walls, keeping the hunched figure in front of them.

It's not hard to follow her because she never stops and turns round to look.

Joel has always believed that people

who are being followed can sense it. But evidently not Gertrud. No-Nose. People either feel sorry for Gertrud, or dislike her. But nearly everybody is frightened of her.

You can feel sorry for her because she lost her nose during an operation at the hospital. You can also dislike her because she doesn't stay indoors but wanders around in the street and doesn't cover up her deformed face.

She must be brave, and everybody's frightened of brave people.

When Joel sees her in the street he thinks it's both disgusting and exciting to see her face without a nose.

She usually has a white handkerchief stuffed into the hole where her nose should be.

Every time he sees her he tells himself he's not going to look, but he can't resist it.

She goes to the Pentecostal chapel next to the Community Centre. She patrols the streets every day, selling religious magazines. Hardly anybody dares not to stop and buy one off her.

He knows she tried to drown herself

in the river when they'd cut off her nose at the hospital. But somebody saw her jump in, and rowed out in the horse dealer's boat and rescued her. She'd had a heavy iron in her pocket and a thick chain wrapped round her neck. Then Happy Harry, the Pentecostal minister, took her under his wing, and now she sells magazines for him.

She lives all alone, in a little house at Ulvkälla, on the far side of the bridge. That seems to be where she's heading for.

They follow her as far as the bridge. Then it gets hard, because there are so many lights on the bridge. They watch her disappear into the shadows.

Joel tells Ture what he knows about her. When he's finished, Ture asks a peculiar question.

'Do you know where there's an ants' nest?' he asks.

An ants' nest?

Joel knows where there are lots of ants' nests, but they are all still covered in snow. The ants don't usually emerge until May.

'We'll pay her a visit tomorrow,' says Ture. 'I want to go home now.'

'You said you were going to show me something,' says Joel.

'I have done,' says Ture. 'How to trail a person.'

Joel goes with Ture as far as his gate. He hopes Ture will invite him to call round after school, but Ture says nothing. He simply jumps over the gate and vanishes into his vast house.

Joel has the feeling that Ture is already beginning to take over The Secret Society.

That's a good thing but also a bad thing.

What is good is that Joel no longer has sole responsibility for it all. But what is bad is that everything has happened so quickly.

He hurries home. It's freezing, and he feels cold. He can hear The Old Bricklayer's lorry somewhere in the distance. When he enters the kitchen he has the same feeling as the night before. There's something amiss. This time it's even stronger.

He feels scared. What has changed?

He unlaces his boots and hangs up his jacket. Everything is the same as usual, but at the same time, it's different.

Without really knowing why, he opens the door to his father's room. He knows exactly how far he can open it before it starts creaking.

He listens for his dad's breathing. But he hears nothing.

Just for a moment he's so scared that he almost bursts into tears. Has Samuel died?

He gropes his way forward. It's pitch black, but even so he closes his eyes.

Breathe, he thinks. Breathe, breathe, breathe . . .

He knocks against the side of the bed with his knee.

He has to open his eyes now. He must face up to the most difficult task he's ever been landed with.

Face up to something he doesn't really dare face up to.

His eyes fail to respond.

His eyelids are secured by heavy padlocks.

Big dogs are running back and forth,

preventing him from opening his eyes.

But in the end he forces his eyes open, as if he'd used dynamite to set himself free.

Despite the darkness he can see that the bed is empty.

His father has abandoned him.

6

What actually happened that night when Joel discovered that his father was not in his bed?

He wasn't at all sure. All his memories were blurred, as if he'd been looking at unfocused photos, when he tried to remember later. What he would really like to do was to forget that night altogether; but his memory was stronger than the urge to forget, and his fear was so great that he couldn't shake it off.

What happened?

What did he do?

He sat quite still on the edge of his father's bed and cried his eyes out.

That deadened his fear. Then he ran round and round the empty flat, as if he were suffering severe pains that he was trying to shake off.

All the time he kept thinking he could hear Samuel's footsteps on the stairs, but when he flung open the door there was nobody there. He looked out of the window but the street was deserted, and the night glared disdainfully back at him.

And he thought lots of awful thoughts.

First he'd been abandoned by his mother. Now his father had done the same thing to him.

The good humour, humming the sea shanties, promising to buy him a bike—it had all been false.

His fear was so great, he could hear it bellowing deep down in his subconscious. As if there were a dog chained up inside him, howling non-stop.

It was a long time before he calmed down sufficiently to think straight again.

There were no trains running at

night. They didn't have a car. And Samuel could hardly have set out for the far side of the vast forest on foot.

There was only one explanation and Joel felt he needed to have immediate confirmation of what he knew was true.

As he runs down the stairs again, the door to old Mrs Westman's flat opens and she stands there framed by the light coming from her hall, wearing a brown dressing gown and a white nightcap.

'It's shocking, all this running up and down stairs,' she says. 'Has something happened?'

'No,' says Joel. 'Nothing at all.'

It occurs to him that it might be a good idea to hide in Mrs Westman's flat. Hide behind all her embroidered pictures of Christ in the flat smelling of apples, and pretend that he doesn't exist. But he runs out into the street and keeps on running.

He doesn't stop until he gets to the entrance door of the block of flats where Sara lives. He's been running so fast that he has a stitch, and the cold air is biting into his throat.

He opens the door carefully and sneaks into the dark rear courtyard. There is a faint light behind the curtains in one of Sara's windows.

He looks round the courtyard but can't see a ladder. He knows there is one behind the ironmonger's on the other side of the street, so he runs back through the entrance door, over the street, and sees the ladder half-buried under the snow. It's heavy. He can hardly lift it. He has to use all his strength to lug it over the street.

Jesus with the cross, he thinks. Jesus with the cross and Joel with the ladder . . .

By the time he's carried the ladder into Sara's rear courtyard, he's soaked in sweat. His bladder is bursting, and he pees all over the bicycle he thinks belongs to Sara. There is still a faint light behind one of the curtains. He's shivering with cold, and tries to work out how best to raise the ladder and lean it against the wall without making a noise.

But he can't think of any way. The

ladder is too heavy. He'll just have to try to slide it up the wall and hope nobody hears anything.

Not that it matters. Nothing matters any more.

So he braces himself, heaves with all his strength and manages to raise the ladder against the wall.

No sign of movement behind the curtain.

He's out of breath and sweaty, and his throat feels raw.

But the worst is yet to come.

He climbs tentatively up the ladder until his head is almost up to the windowsill.

He closes his eyes; once again his eyelids are padlocked. He's prepared to give up everything—The Flying Horse, *Celestine*, his rock—as long as Samuel isn't behind the curtain.

Then he looks.

Sara is lying under a sheet in a brown bed.

Her mouth is moving, but Joel can't hear what she's saying.

Sitting on the edge of the bed is Samuel.

131

He's naked, and is listening to what Sara has to say.

Through the curtain Joel can see the long, red scar on his father's thigh. The scar he got when a hatch burst open in a severe storm off the Hebrides, and he almost lost a leg.

He's giving that scar to Sara . . .

Joel is overcome by a deep sense of pain and sorrow as he perches there on the ladder. It's as if he no longer exists, as if he were condemned to perch on that ladder, frozen stiff, for a thousand years.

Why has he been abandoned? He's never abandoned anybody. After all, he's his own mum.

He doesn't know how long he stands there on the ladder. But he doesn't climb down until his sorrow has slowly given way to contempt and fury.

He doesn't climb down until he feels strong enough to avenge himself.

He digs out a stone from under the snow next to the wall. It's not very big, only half the size of his fist, but it's big enough.

Now he has to make sure he doesn't

miss.

He'll only have one throw, no more. If he misses and then tries again, he'll be discovered.

It doesn't matter if he is discovered, of course, but he hopes to avoid that even so. He has to hit his target with the first stone. He's not bothered about the ladder. Explaining to the ironmonger how the ladder turned up underneath her window will be even more revenge on Sara.

He takes aim. He's taken his glove off, and holds the cold stone in his frozen hand.

Then he hurls the stone, and feels a pang of regret as he lets go. The stone hits the window right in the middle, and the glass is shattered with a crack that echoes all round the courtyard.

He runs off as fast as he can. He doesn't stop until he's back at home, and the cold air feels like sandpaper in his throat.

When he's got his breath back, he tiptoes cautiously past old Mrs Westman's door.

He wonders if she'll tell his father

that he's been out in the middle of the night.

Samuel will understand what has happened if she does.

But the thought only worries Joel a little bit.

He turns on all the lights in the flat before untying his boots with his freezing cold fingers. One of the laces has got a knot that he can't unravel. He fetches the bread knife and cuts it off. He undresses and snuggles down into bed in order to warm up.

He's not going to think about his father as such any more. From now on he will call him Samuel.

It strikes him it was silly to leave the lights on. He switches them all off then creeps back into bed. Then he waits, waits for Samuel to come back home. But he's so tired, he can't keep his eyes open and he nods off to sleep.

His dreams are restless, nasty, long-drawn-out. Dreams he won't remember anything about . . .

When he wakes up next morning Samuel has already left for the forest. Joel stands in the kitchen doorway and sees that he has been there and made coffee. The stove is still hot.

The bootlace Joel had cut off is lying on the floor like a strip of a shed snakeskin.

Joel is tired. He must hurry up if he's going to get to school on time.

But when he emerges into the cold dawn he decides that he's not going to go to school. He can't face it, he has to do some thinking. Mind you, it's not sure that he'll have the strength to think either. It would be good if he had a tap inside his head that he could open, and let all his thoughts run out . . .

For no obvious reason he finds himself heading north out of the little town. First the long hill up to the railway station. Beyond that is the hospital, and then the endless forest.

In a little hollow by the road, almost completely hemmed in by dense fir trees, is The Old Bricklayer's house. It's a dilapidated smithy that has been converted into a private home. The garden is full of junk and overgrown currant bushes.

Joel pauses and peers in through the dense fir trees. He can see wheel tracks in the snow. Then somebody shouts to him.

'Come here,' somebody says. 'Come and give me a hand.'

He looks round. He can see nothing but trees. Fir trees with a thick covering of snow on their branches.

'I need a hand,' he hears the voice say once more.

And then he sees The Old Bricklayer, in among the fir trees.

He waves to him.

'Come over here and hold this,' shouts The Old Bricklayer.

Joel approaches hesitantly.

The Old Bricklayer emerges from the trees with the end of a thick, long rope in one hand.

Joel thinks that his real name is so appropriate. A man with a name like Simon Windstorm has to look exactly like The Old Bricklayer. He has big gaps in his mouth—no doubt his teeth have blown away. Bushy eyebrows are sprouting round his eyes like rambling rose bushes. His eyes are bright and piercing, and he seems to be looking right through Joel.

The Old Bricklayer is wearing a voluminous fur coat riddled with large moth-holes. He has a Wellington boot on one foot, and a spiked boot on the other.

The Old Bricklayer notices that Joel is intrigued.

'You're looking at my feet, are you?' he says. 'People have no idea of what's best. I can slide forward using my Wellington, and use the spiked boot to dig into the ice and keep me steady. Who says you have to have identical boots on both feet? Does it say anything about that in the Bible? Do the police have the right to arrest people who wear odd boots? Of course not. Not even any two feet are the same. Hang on to this rope now!'

He stuffs the end of the rope into Joel's hands and vanishes again into the trees. The rope becomes taut, and The Old Bricklayer comes hurrying back through the snow.

It strikes Joel that he looks like an animal. A sort of cross between an elk and a human being. A Windstorm Ox.

He takes the rope from Joel and lays it down in the snow so that it stays taut. All the time he's mumbling and snorting to himself.

'What are you doing?' Joel asks.

The Old Bricklayer looks at him in surprise.

'Doing?' he says. 'I'm laying out the rope in the snow. I think it looks good. I only do things that look good.'

Then he looks worried.

'Do you think it looks good?'

'Of course,' says Joel. 'It looks really good . . .'

The Old Bricklayer lies down in the snow and relaxes, as if he were lying in the warm heather on a summer's day.

'I feel less isolated when I do something that looks good,' he says. 'That's my medicine. I was ill for a long time. It was only when I started doing things that look good that I started to be healthy again.'

The man's mad, Joel thinks. No normal person lays out ropes in the snow and thinks it looks good.

'The earth is round,' says The Old

Bricklayer. 'It spins round and round. Sometimes I get dizzy and I have to lie down in the snow, and cool my head down. Then I can think about the past and the future. And while all that stuff's going on, I'm alive. When I'm dead I won't be alive any longer. That's the top and bottom of it. But I'm a bit worried when I think that nobody will realise how important it is to lay ropes out in the snow when I've gone. I wish I had some apprentices ...'

'Why do you drive around in your lorry at night?' asks Joel, hoping that The Old Bricklayer will recognise Joel as the boy he helped out of the snow when The Flying Horse had crashed.

But Simon Windstorm doesn't recognise him. He lies in the snow, gazing up at the sky.

'I've given up sleeping,' he says. 'There's nothing so lonely for a lonely man as sleeping alone in a lonely house. So I get into my lorry and drive round. I think about all those years I was in hospital, and I sing to banish all the nasty memories. You can sing away your sorrows. And you can whistle away your nasty memories so that they don't dare come back . . .'

He suddenly sits up in the snow and looks at Joel.

'Thank you for your help,' he says. 'You can go now. I want to be left in peace. But come back some other time and I'll give you some soup that will enable you to see into the future.'

'That's not possible,' says Joel.

'Oh yes it is,' says The Old Bricklayer. 'Come back to see me, and I'll show you.'

Then he gets up, brushes off the snow and plods off into the trees.

Joel continues on his way.

He tries out what The Old Bricklayer said, to find out if it's true. That you can sing away the things you'd rather not think about.

He knows 'Shenandoah' off by heart.

He thinks about Sara with her red hat, and starts singing, loudly and out of tune.

After the first verse she is still patting him on the cheek. After the second verse, that he can't really remember

140

properly, she is starting to fade away. After the third verse she's disappeared altogether. But as soon as he finishes, she comes back again. I can't remember the words, he thinks. It doesn't help ...

He goes back home to his house by the river. It starts snowing, and it's hard going.

I have to speak to him today, he thinks. Samuel. If he tells me where Jenny is, he can sit on Sara's bed and show her his scar as much as he likes.

Although he prefers not to think about it, he does realise that when Samuel sits naked on the edge of her bed, that means he could end up with unwanted brothers and sisters.

Sisters, he thinks. It would be bound to be sisters. Little Saras with red hats ...

He stamps hard as he tramps up the stairs. The sound echoes from wall to wall and he knows that Mrs Westman won't like the noise, but at least being able to hear his footsteps proves that he still exists.

He lights the stove and watches the

flames licking the wood. He sticks a finger inside and tests how long he can keep it there without getting burnt.

Then he decides to search Samuel's room. The photographs must be there somewhere. Now he will find them.

Samuel's room has a bed and a chair. A table with the radio on it and a bookcase full of books. His clothes are hanging in a wardrobe. Nothing else in there. Joel looks round and asks himself where he would hide some photographs. But he knows that strangely enough, adults don't think like children. They often find worse hiding places.

He starts by looking in bad hiding places. Under the pillow, between the bookcase and the wall, under the carpet. Nothing there. He shakes all the books, but no photographs drop out. Then he searches through the table drawer where Samuel keeps his penknife with the mother-of-pearl handle among lots of papers, and his sailor's record book. No photographs there either.

So Samuel hasn't chosen a bad hiding place. He has to think again.

Good hiding places are places you don't think of as hiding places. Places you don't see, don't even notice that they exist. A good hiding place could be underneath a newspaper.

He lifts up the newspaper but there's only dust underneath.

Another good hiding place could be underneath the embroidered table mat Samuel was given by Mrs Westman.

He lifts up the cloth. There are the photographs. But not only the photographs: also a letter. He takes the photos and the letter to the window seat in the hall where he can keep an eye on the street and see Samuel coming in good time.

He examines the photos carefully, but he doesn't think he looks all that much like his mother. He fetches Samuel's shaving mirror from the bathroom and holds it so that he can see Jenny's face and his own at the same time.

Perhaps there is a bit of a likeness after all? He tries to pose in the same

143

way as his mother. Moves his lips backwards and forwards, raises an eyebrow, blows out his cheeks a little. In the end he thinks he has adjusted his face to ape his mother's. Now he can see that there is a likeness. Not a lot, but it is there.

Then he remembers that he hasn't been keeping an eye on the street. Two small children run past, a bus signals that it's turning left. But there's no sign of Samuel trudging home from the forest. He puts the photographs on the window ledge and looks at the letter. He sees that it is postmarked in Gothenburg. November 19. But he can't make out the year.

He takes the letter out of its envelope. It's folded in two and written in ink on both sides.

To his surprise he sees that it is written by Samuel. 'Your ever-loving Samuel', it says at the bottom of page two. He examines the envelope.

'To Samuel Gustafson, The Seafarer Guest House, Gothenburg.'

Does he write letters to himself? Joel wonders.

He looks out over the street. It's snowing heavily now, big chunky flakes. The errand boy from the sawmill is going past, carrying a parcel. Joel notices that he keeps changing hands. It must be heavy.

He reads what Samuel has written.

It's a letter to Joel's mother.

He writes that this very day he has signed on with the SS *Vassijaure* that has been in the shipyard to have its propeller shaft changed. Tomorrow they will sail for Narvik and pick up a cargo of iron ore for taking to Newport News. He doesn't know the next port of call but he hopes it will be somewhere in Sweden so that he can take a few days' leave and visit her in Motala. Then he tells her that he has backache but expects it will soon pass, and that somebody he knows called Lundström has signed on for the same ship. He asks if Jenny remembers Lundström. He had a long beard and used to play the concertina. He tells her how much he misses her, and that she must stay faithful to him . . .

Joel reads the letter one more time,

after checking to make sure Samuel isn't approaching the house.

There is a lot in the letter that gives him food for thought.

The most important thing is Motala. He fetches his diary, which contains a map of Sweden, and locates the town. It's almost in the very middle of the country.

Perhaps that's where his mother returned to when she left?

But why is the letter in the wrong envelope?

Why does Samuel have a letter that she ought to have had?

Perhaps Simon Windstorm has some kind of potion that enables you to see into the past, Joel thinks. He could do with something of the sort.

He notices that the fire in the stove has gone out. He hurries to replace the letter and photographs, and puts the shaving mirror back in the bathroom.

As he is relighting the fire he realises that he can almost remember the contents of the letter by heart.

SS *Vassijaure*, The Seafarer Guest

House, Motala . . .

He lays the table while the potatoes are boiling. He sees through the window that the snow is falling thicker than ever. It's starting to get dark. He goes to the window seat again and waits. Black figures pass by through the snow.

And there comes Samuel.

Joel can tell from the way he's walking that he's in a good mood.

He jumps down from the window seat and goes to his room. He doesn't want Samuel to see that he's been looking out for him. He rummages under his bed and produces his tin soldiers, covered in dust.

Then Samuel appears in the doorway. He laughs and brandishes a piece of meat in his hand.

'We'll be eating well tonight,' he says. Then he lowers his voice.

'Elk steak. But don't tell anybody. It's not allowed at this time of year. But it's good!'

Joel sits on the kitchen bench and watches Samuel turning the meat in the frying pan.

It's not easy to understand grown-ups. Sometimes they stand over you and want to know everything, but just as often they don't want to know anything at all.

Joel likes elk meat. It has a very special taste. Besides, you can eat as much lingonberry jam with it as you want. When there is elk meat on the table Samuel never bothers to frown if Joel takes too much jam.

They eat in silence. Samuel rarely speaks at the dinner table. He just eats. Joel knows that the best time to ask something is when they've just finished eating, before Samuel has fetched the newspaper he has in his overcoat pocket and lies down on the kitchen bench or sits down on his chair and starts reading.

The trick is to have your question ready when Samuel pushes his plate to one side and wipes his mouth.

'I dreamt about my mother last night,' he says when Samuel puts down his knife and fork.

'Really?' he says. 'What did you dream?'

'I can't remember,' says Joel. 'But I know it was her I dreamt about.'

'It would be just like her to start haunting you in your dreams,' says Samuel, and now he sounds annoyed.

'Why?' asks Samuel.

'You shouldn't think so much about your mother,' says Samuel. 'I understand that it's not so easy for you not to have a mum, but she was no good. She wasn't the person I thought she was.'

'What was she like, then?' asks Joel.

Samuel looks long and hard at him.

'We can talk about that when you're a bit bigger,' he says, getting up from the table.

'How much bigger?' wonders Joel.

Samuel doesn't answer but goes to fetch his newspaper.

When he comes back he pauses and looks at Joel.

'No doubt you think your mother was a wonderful person,' he says. 'I don't want to disappoint you. We can talk about her when you're a bit bigger.'

Then he goes to his room leaving Joel on his own at the table.

149

'Disappoint you', he thinks.

What does Samuel—the man he no longer calls father—know about Joel's disappointments?

Nothing ...

If he goes to Sara again tonight, I shall run away, he thinks.

He stays in his room all evening. He moves his tin soldiers back and forth without paying any attention to what he's doing.

He wonders if Ture will be able to help him scare Sara off.

It's hardly going to be possible to scare Samuel. How can you scare somebody who doesn't understand anything?

If he knew what Joel was thinking, he wouldn't bother about Sara of course ... It occurs to him that there might be another possibility.

What if he were to go and see Sara himself? Go to the bar and tell her to leave Samuel alone. Tell her that he was the one who threw that stone, and that he doesn't want any sisters with red hats.

Maybe she would understand that it

was important. After all, she had a boy herself who was killed in a fire.

He goes to bed and thinks that might be the best solution. He'll go to the bar and talk to Sara.

Suddenly Samuel appears in the doorway.

He comes to sit on Joel's bed. He smiles, but it seems to Joel that the smile isn't anything to do with him, but because Samuel is thinking about Sara.

'Would you like to hear a sea story?' asks Samuel.

Joel would really, but he forces himself to say no.

'I'm nearly asleep already,' he says.

'Sleep well, then,' says Samuel. 'Maybe tomorrow . . .'

Joel wraps the alarm clock in a sock and places it under his pillow. He wishes he didn't have to get up tonight. If he doesn't turn up at school tomorrow Miss Nederström will start wondering what's going on.

Best of all would be to sleep right through until summer. Wake up and know that it was the summer holidays and that Sara had moved to somewhere a long way away. If only it were possible just once to wish for something it was impossible to wish for . . .

Even so he is happy when the alarm goes off and he wakes up. The first thing he hears is Samuel snoring next door. So he hasn't gone to see Sara tonight.

Perhaps that stone through the window was enough, he thinks. Perhaps Samuel will never go there again?

Now he no longer feels tired.

Perhaps everything can be just like it used to be?

He gets dressed, goes downstairs and out into the night.

It's not as cold as it has been, so it doesn't hurt when he breathes.

Spring is on its way, he thinks. First comes spring, and then the summer holidays . . .

Ture is waiting for him by the goods wagons. He has a spade with him, and a paper sack.

The ant hill, thinks Joel. He'd forgotten about that.

152

But why does Ture want Joel to show him an ant hill?

Next to the sawmill there's a clump of trees with lots of ant hills. Maybe the snow isn't so deep there.

Joel takes the paper sack and they hurry off. As usual everything is quiet and deserted.

As they pass the church they see the rear lights of The Old Bricklayer's lorry as it turns into Hedevägen.

Next to the roots of a fallen tree they find an ant hill with not much snow covering it.

Ture has brought a torch so that they can pick their way through the trees. Joel thinks that he wouldn't have dared come here by himself, even if he'd had a torch. The trees are too tall, the loneliness is too oppressive away from the streetlights.

'Hold the torch,' whispers Ture.

Then he starts digging at the bottom of the ant hill. It takes him a long time to hack his way through the frozen soil, the pine needles and the hibernating ants.

Joel holds the sack open so that Ture

153

can fill it with the pulverised soil. Then they change places and Joel has a go at digging.

What's he going to do with all this? Joel wonders as he hacks away at the frozen soil and tree roots. Why does he want sleeping ants and frozen soil?

When the torch batteries start to wear out, they pack up and leave.

On the other side of the bridge Joel turns off and takes a road that meanders past silent houses.

Eventually he stops and points.

This is where Gertrud lives.

It's a little yellow wooden house all on its own at the end of the road. In the garden are currant bushes and a potato patch.

Ture stands the spade in a snowdrift.

The house is in darkness.

'Does she have a dog?' whispers Ture.

Joel shakes his head. 'Not that I know of.'

'Wait here,' says Ture and slinks in through the gate, which isn't properly closed. He vanishes into the darkness.

Joel suddenly starts feeling uneasy.

What is Ture going to do?

After a few minutes Ture reappears. He looks pleased with himself. He gestures to Joel to bring the sack and follow him.

At the back of the house there is a window standing ajar. Ture has put a crate underneath it that they can stand on. Ture carefully opens the window wide.

'Pass me the sack,' he whispers.

There is a table just inside the window.

Ture tips the frozen soil and the sleeping ants onto the table. When the sack is empty he carefully closes the window again.

'There we go,' he says.

He puts the crate back where it was, then they hurry back over the railway bridge.

Ture laughs.

'By the time she wakes up tomorrow the ants will have thawed out,' he says. 'The whole house will be crawling with ants.'

Joel laughs as well.

In fact he's not at all sure that he likes this. It's one thing throwing a stone through Sara's window. He knows why he did that. But tipping ants through No-Nose's window? Why?

To create fear, Ture has said.

But why create fear in No-Nose?

'Tomorrow we'll smear varnish all over her currant bushes,' says Ture. 'This is just the start.'

Smear varnish over her currant bushes?

That's not something Joel would ever have thought of doing.

This isn't what his Secret Society was set up to do.

The dog heading for a star no longer seems to be a part of it.

'I want to look for the dog,' he says. 'I don't want to smear varnish over any currant bushes.'

'You daren't,' says Ture.

'Of course I dare,' says Joel. 'But I don't want to.'

Then they start quarrelling.

Neither of them says anything, but they quarrel even so, in their thoughts.

They walk all the way home without saying a word.

They go their different ways when they get to the courthouse gate.

'See you tomorrow,' says Ture and jumps over the gate.

Joel doesn't answer, but hands over the paper sack. Ture has been carrying the spade.

'I have to go home now,' says Joel. 'I can't spend all tomorrow in bed.'

He has no intention of smearing varnish over any currant bushes, he intends to look for the dog. But he doesn't say that.

On the way home he thinks about Ture running away soon. Then Joel will be alone again with his Secret Society. At least he won't have to do things he doesn't want to do any more.

Such as smearing varnish on currant bushes.

It's not that he's a coward, he dares to do it all right. It's just that he doesn't want to.

When he enters the kitchen he can sense straight away that Samuel isn't asleep in his bed. He doesn't need to

157

check if Samuel's clothes and boots are still there. He knows even so.

He edges open the door to Samuel's room. The bed is empty. Joel starts crying. He sits on the kitchen bench with tears running down his cheeks. He sits there for ages.

Then he takes out the logbook from underneath *Celestine*. He finds a pen and writes on an empty page: 'All the crew have been lost now. The last one to be swept overboard was Able Seaman Samuel Gustafson. His son fought to the last to save him, but it was all in vain.

The only one left on board now is Joel Gustafson.

No other soul, only Joel Gustafson . . .'

7

When Joel wakes up next morning and goes to the kitchen, he sees that Samuel has not been at home all night. The stove is cold and there is no dirty coffee cup in the sink.

He is gripped by fear once again. It's a monster inside his stomach. An animal with vicious teeth and sharp claws, a beast eating its fill inside frightened people.

Joel decides to go out, lie down in the forest and die.

Samuel is not going to return.

He has gone away just like his mother did, and left Joel behind. He didn't even bother to take his son down to Mrs Westman's and leave him there.

He tries to convince himself that this isn't the case, and that he's only imagining it, but to believe that he'd have to ignore the cold stove and the coffee cup that isn't where it usually is.

He can't do that. There's a limit to

how far he can go to fool himself.

He gets dressed and goes out into the street. It's colder again and steam comes out of his mouth when he breathes.

He can't go to school. That's out of the question. Everybody would be able to see by looking at him that Samuel had abandoned him and moved in with Sara, the waitress in the local bar. He makes up his mind to go so far into the forest that he won't be able to find his way back, and so can't have any second thoughts.

The forest is most extensive to the north, he knows that. There are also a lot of deep ravines and black tarns there. Lots of people have lost their way in that part of the forest and never returned. Now he'll become one of them. The difference being that he'll get lost on purpose.

He goes up the hill to the railway station, thinking that this is the last time. He turns round halfway up and surveys his own footprints. He remembers that his name is carved into the rock down by the river.

That will still be there when he's gone.

What has happened seems so unfair. How can you blame yourself when you can't choose your own parents?

And why would Sara want to choose Samuel? Or is it Samuel who's chosen her?

Perhaps he thinks I've been a bad mum to myself, Joel muses.

Maybe he thinks I've been just as bad as Jenny.

He stops when he comes to the road leading to Simon Windstorm's house.

Perhaps he can have a taste of Simon's soup before he goes to get lost in the forest? If it's true that it will enable him to see into the future, he'll be able to find out what happens after he's dead.

He walks through the dense fir trees, follows the lorry tracks and finds himself in the forecourt. Rusty machines, dismantled motor cars and power-looms are lying around everywhere, part-covered in snow.

It's like a cemetery, he thinks. Although the gravestones are rusty machines and don't have names carved on them.

He looks at the dilapidated house. There is no smoke coming out of the chimney, not a sound to be heard.

He approaches one of the windows and peers inside. The Old Bricklayer is sitting at a table, reading a book. He has a pen in one hand, and occasionally writes something in the book.

Suddenly, he looks up, straight at Joel, and waves to him. Joel hears Simon inviting him inside.

When Joel takes hold of the door handle he notices that it turns the wrong way, the opposite way to all other door handles he's ever come across. He enters a murky vestibule smelling of tar. A pile of newspapers reaches up to the ceiling. There's also a tailor's dummy dressed in an old fur coat.

The room where The Old Bricklayer is sitting smells of smoke oozing out of a stove. A few hens are pecking at the rag carpets.

'I have some soup for you,' says The

Old Bricklayer with a smile. 'I heard you coming.'

'How could you possibly hear me?' asks Joel.

The Old Bricklayer points into a corner of the room. There's a dog lying there, looking at Joel. A Norwegian elkhound . . .

But it's not the dog that's heading for a star. It's similar, but not the same.

'Lukas hears everything,' says The Old Bricklayer. 'Sit down now.' Joel sits down at the table on a peculiar chair. It's really two chairs but their backs are nailed to each other.

'What are you reading?' he asks.

'I've no idea what books are called,' says The Old Bricklayer. 'I read bits here and there and if there's something I don't like, I change it. This book has an ending I don't like, so I'm writing a new one as I want it to be.'

'Are you allowed to do that?' asks Joel.

The Old Bricklayer gives him a long, hard look.

'There are all sorts of things you're

not supposed to do,' he says. 'You're not supposed to wear odd shoes, you're not supposed to live in an old smithy, you're not supposed to have hens in the house. No doubt you're not supposed to make changes in books either. But I do all that even so. I'm not doing anybody any harm. Besides, I'm mad.'

'Are you?' asks Joel.

'No doubt I was once,' he says. 'All thoughts I had caused me so much pain. But that's all changed now. Now I only think thoughts that I like. But I suppose I'm a little bit mad.'

'You said you were going to serve me your soup,' says Joel. 'I need to know what's going to happen this afternoon and this evening.'

The Old Bricklayer gives him another long, hard look.

'You don't look too happy,' he says eventually. 'You look as if you have a lot of thoughts in your head that you would prefer not to be there. Is that right?'

Joel nods.

'Yes,' he says. 'I suppose so.'

Joel starts to tell The Old Bricklayer all about it. The words simply tumble out of his mouth, with no hesitation. He tells him about his dad, who he now just calls Samuel, about his mother and *Celestine*, about The Secret Society and Sara in the bar. He tells him about the stone he threw through her window, and about the dog that's heading for a star.

He's sure The Old Bricklayer is listening to what he has to say. He's not the type who just pretends to be listening.

When Joel finishes speaking it is remarkably quiet in the room. The only sound is from the hens' beaks pecking at the floor.

'You and I are going for a ride in my lorry,' says The Old Bricklayer, getting to his feet. 'There's something I want to show you.'

Joel clambers into the cab. He's never been in a lorry before. The Old Bricklayer gets in behind the wheel, turns a key and pulls a knob. But the engine doesn't start.

'Go and give the bonnet a bash with

this,' he says, handing Joel a hammer.

'Where exactly?' asks Joel.

'Where you see the dents,' says The Old Bricklayer. 'Hit it as hard as you can and don't stop until I tell you to.'

Joel does as he's bidden and the engine springs into life. Why on earth does it start when he hits the bonnet with a hammer?

He clambers back into the cab. A hen suddenly appears from behind the seat and flutters out through the open door.

'Ah, I wondered where she'd got to,' mutters The Old Bricklayer. 'In the summer they usually come to lay eggs behind the seats.'

They drive out to the main road and head north.

If we'd headed south perhaps he'd have taken me to Motala, thinks Joel. Driven through the forest, night and day, until we got there.

After a few miles The Old Bricklayer slows down and turns off onto a forest track. He doesn't tell Joel what he is going to show him. Joel wishes the journey would never end. The white forest is like a boundless ocean, the lorry a frozen ship forcing its way through the white, icy sea.

A big bird takes off from a fir tree and flies away. Snow cascades down from the branch it has left.

The Old Bricklayer suddenly brings the lorry to a halt. When he switches off the engine Joel experiences a silence he has never come up against before. A thousand trees watching and listening . . .

The Old Bricklayer gazes thoughtfully through the windscreen.

'Time for walking now,' he says, hopping down from the cab.

Joel trudges after him through the deep snow. The firs are lined up side by side, and Joel wonders where they are heading for. But he feels secure with The Old Bricklayer at his side. Everything he's heard about him before, all the scary rumours, have been banished.

The forest suddenly opens up and a white lake, covered in ice and snow, is revealed before them. The firs crowd in on it, restlessly, on all sides. In the middle of the lake is something jutting up: Joel thinks it's a rock, but when he ventures out onto the snow-covered ice he sees that it is in fact a rowing boat, frozen in.

They walk over to it. The Old Bricklayer adjusts the oars and rowlocks lying in the bottom of the boat. There are also a couple of collapsible canvas stools of the type used by men who fish through holes in the ice as spring approaches.

The Old Bricklayer sets them up on the ice. He sits on one of them and indicates to Joel that he should do the same.

'This lake doesn't have a name on the map,' says The Old Bricklayer. 'But I've given it one. A secret name. Four Winds Lake. I'll tell you why it's called that ...

'The first time I ever came here,' says The Old Bricklayer, 'I was very mixed-up. I'd just come back home after having lived in a hospital where people whose heads were full of horrible thoughts were locked up behind doors and barred windows. I was so pleased to have been released at last. Nevertheless I was sad because I was all alone and had spent far too many years hidden away in that hospital. I came out here into the forest and discovered this lake. It was in the winter, just like now, and I stood on the ice, more or less where we are sitting now, and then I shouted out my name as loud as I possibly could, Simon. Simon, I shouted. I don't know why I did that. It just happened. But when I'd finished shouting it seemed that all four winds came blowing from out of the forest. One from each point of the compass. One of the winds was cold, and whispered, "Sorrow, Sorrow" in my ear. Another one whined and growled, "Fury, Fury" in my ear. The third one was warm and winged its way gently to my ear and whispered, "Happiness, Happiness." The fourth wind was both warm and cold, and at first I couldn't hear what it was saying, but in the end I realised that it was telling me to choose which wind I wanted to have blowing at my face. I turned my back on all the other winds and let Happiness stroke my cheeks. It felt as if the sorrow I'd been feeling had just melted away. And when I left, I felt so happy. I come back here whenever I need to listen to the winds. It's like a fairy tale, this lake. Perhaps it is a fairy tale. Perhaps the winds don't really exist. But even if they don't, they still help. I reckon they might be able to help you in the same way that they helped me. Now I'm going back to the lorry, and I'll wait for you there. You have to be on your own if the winds are going to dare to appear. All you need to do is to shout your name, then wait.'

The Old Bricklayer stands up and collapses his stool.

'I'll be waiting in the lorry,' he says. 'You'll be able to find your way back. You can't miss our tracks in the snow.'

The Old Bricklayer leaves and vanishes into the dark fir trees. Joel is on his own.

There's no such things as talking winds, he thinks. It's only in fairy tales that stones can laugh and flowers can turn into pretty maids all in a row.

170

There are no winds capable of whispering into his ear.

Still, there's no harm in shouting your name, I suppose. Even if you don't believe that anything can possibly come of it. You can shout out your name and see if there's an echo.

He shouts his name.

It sounds so short, so solitary. Like somebody calling for a cat or a cow. There's no echo either.

He shouts again, louder this time.

No wind from the forest. Everything is still.

But he imagines the wind inside himself. You can do that. You can create a wind that doesn't exist if you really have to.

It's like holding one of Samuel's shells to your ear and thinking that the rushing sound is a voice.

A beam of sunlight emerges from the clouds, just over the tops of the trees. If he turns to face the sun, it feels quite warm on his face. The idea of lying down in the snow to die suddenly seems absolutely impossible.

How could he ever have thought of

such a thing?

He feels almost embarrassed. It's childish, he thinks. Going out into the forest to die is childish. You can't get lost on purpose.

The secret of this lake suddenly dawns on him.

Maybe the four winds don't exist. But the very fact that they don't exist makes you start thinking differently from the way you thought before.

Now he wants to get back home, fast. No doubt it will be easier to talk to Samuel today. He must have grown tired of Sara in the red hat by now.

He folds up the canvas stool, puts it back into the rowing boat and retraces his steps. The fir trees come to greet him, and he leaps into their shadow as if into a welcoming tunnel.

There's the lorry. The engine is coughing and wheezing, and he can see The Old Bricklayer sitting behind the wheel. He opens the door and climbs up into the passenger seat.

'All OK?' asks The Old Bricklayer.

Joel nods.

'I'd better be getting home now,' he

says.

The Old Bricklayer drives him to his front gate.

'You didn't have any soup,' says The Old Bricklayer.

'I'll come some other time,' says Joel.

'Maybe,' says The Old Bricklayer, with a smile. Then he drives off.

As he bounds up the stairs he wonders if Simon Windstorm recognised him. Did he realise that Joel was the boy who'd fallen off his bike that night in the snow? Maybe it's more interesting not to know, he thinks.

When he opens the flat door it's obvious that Samuel is already at home. He shouldn't be. It's not late enough in the day for him to have finished work. Joel can see that he's in a serious mood.

I'm rumbled, Joel thought. He knows I was the one who threw the stone, he knows that I haven't been to school, he knows everything . . .

Now Joel will have to watch his step. Samuel can get very angry, especially if his son tells lies. Nevertheless Joel will have to try to find out precisely what Samuel knows and what he doesn't know. Unless it's necessary, a full admission won't be called for.

But Joel is wrong. It's not what he thinks at all.

'There's been an accident,' says Samuel. 'Somebody was hit by a falling tree. We had to take him to hospital by horse, but it was too late.'

It has happened once before that one of Samuel's workmates died in an accident. On that occasion he stayed at home for days, studying his sea charts, before going back into the forest again.

It strikes Joel that his father looks like a little boy, sitting on the kitchen bench with his big fists clenched on the table in front of him. His hands are large and rough, but even so they look small. Hands can look sad as well.

Joel takes off his boots and jacket and sits down on his chair.

If I console him he'll realise that he and I are the ones who belong together, he thinks. Not Samuel and Sara.

The stove is cold. Joel stands up and

starts loading it with paper and firewood. He keeps an eye on Samuel all the time, but he's still sitting with his little fists on the table in front of him, staring at the cloth.

Joel lights the fire and puts on some water for coffee.

'He's dead now,' says Samuel. 'This morning he got out of bed and made coffee. He had no idea he was going to go into the forest and die, Evert Petterson . . .'

He raises his head and looks at Joel. His helplessness makes him seem so small. Just as small as when he's spent some nights scrubbing away his demons. Just as small as when he's been drinking and stays in bed punishing himself.

'The forest is no place to be,' says Joel. 'Why don't we move away from here? Why don't you become a sailor again? Next time it'll be your head the tree falls down onto. What shall I do then? Move in with old Mrs Westman downstairs? Or go and live with Sara?'

He hadn't intended to say that last bit. The words just came tumbling out.

But Samuel doesn't react. He just continues looking miserable.

'I've thought about that, in fact,' he says. 'About what will happen to you if anything happens to me. I've thought about that ...'

'I'm not moving in with Sara,' says Joel. 'I'd rather live with Simon Windstorm.'

Samuel looks at him in surprise.

'Whatever for?' he says. 'The man's mad ...'

'He's not mad at all,' says Joel. 'I think he's very sensible.'

Samuel shakes his head.

'That's not on,' he says. 'But I have thought about it ...'

'If we move away from here you don't need to think about it,' says Joel. 'There aren't any trees at sea.'

'There are other things at sea,' says Samuel. 'Other things that can fall on your head.'

The water has started boiling on the stove. Joel adds three spoonfuls from the coffee tin and counts slowly to nine, just as Samuel does when he makes coffee. He takes out two cups, one each.

'Do you drink coffee?' asks Samuel. 'I didn't know that.'

'Sometimes,' says Joel. 'Half a cup.'

Samuel gives Joel a funny look. As if Joel were somebody he'd never seen before.

'You're eleven now,' he says. 'Nearly twelve. I keep forgetting that ...'

He stirs his coffee.

It seems to Joel that he has to continue now, when Samuel is in a sorrowful mood, when he doesn't look capable of getting angry.

'I don't like Sara,' he says. 'Why do you keep on seeing her?'

'There's nothing wrong with Sara,' says Samuel. 'She's OK. She puts me in a good mood. She laughs her way through life even though she's endured a lot of things bad enough to make her cry.'

'Don't we laugh, then?' says Joel.

'Don't keep comparing all the time,' says Samuel. 'Sometimes I miss her something terrible, I do so miss ...'

Samuel breaks off without finishing the sentence.

'Mum, Jenny?' suggests Joel.

Samuel nods. Now he seems so small he can barely reach up to the table.

'Of course I miss Jenny,' he says. 'But she ran off. I don't want to miss her. I don't want to miss somebody who doesn't miss me.'

'How do you know that?' asks Joel.

Samuel suddenly grows up and is big again.

'She left me,' he says. 'She ran away from me and you and all the things we were going to do. We were only going to stay here for a few years, while you were little. I was a sailor, this was the only other job I could get at that time. We thought it was a good idea to live here where neither of us had been before. Only for a few years. After that I would sign up with some ship or other again. But then she simply vanishes . . .'

Samuel smashes one of his fists hard down on the table.

'Not a word for all these years,' he says. 'Not a single word. I don't know if she's still alive, or what she's doing . . .'

'She had an itch,' says Joel. 'That's

what Mrs Westman downstairs thinks.'

'Mrs Westman? That old hag downstairs?' says Samuel. 'What does she know about it?'

Joel doesn't know what to do next. He wants to talk about his mother and he wants to talk about Sara, but it's not possible to talk about them both at the same time.

Samuel suddenly stands up.

'I don't want any food,' he says. 'You can make whatever you want for yourself. I know you can. I'm going out for a bit.'

'Don't go to Sara,' Joel begs. 'Don't go to her.'

'I'll go to whoever I want to go to,' says Samuel, glaring at him with a frown.

Joel can see the dangerous glint in his eye.

'Joel,' says Samuel. 'Somebody threw a stone through Sara's window. It wasn't you by any chance, was it?'

Oh yes, thinks Joel. It was me. It was Joel Gustafson who threw that stone. It was Joel Gustafson who lugged the ladder over the street, it was Joel

Gustafson who peeped in through the window and saw Samuel Gustafson sitting naked on Sara's bed, showing off his scar. It was me, Joel Gustafson, who threw that stone and hoped it would hit Sara on the top of her head and that she'd get a bump so big that she couldn't wear that red hat of hers any more . . .

That's what he thinks. But what he says is different.

'No,' he says. 'I haven't been throwing stones.'

Now I must be careful not to look away, he thinks. If I do, Samuel will know it was me.

He looks at Samuel and tries to think about something else. The dog heading for a star. He can think about that.

'I just wondered,' says Samuel. 'But it happened in the middle of the night, so it could hardly have been you. Unless you've started sleepwalking again . . .'

'I haven't been sleepwalking,' says Joel.

Samuel puts on his boots. Then his

leather jacket and his fur hat, in the same order as usual.

'Come with me,' he says out of the blue. 'Come with me to Sara's. I'm sure she'll make you a bite to eat.'

Go with him to Sara's? Joel stares at Samuel. Does he really mean it?

'Come,' says Samuel. 'Let's go together.'

Joel is pleased, thrilled to bits.

But how can he feel pleased when meeting Sara is the last thing he wants to do? He can't understand it.

But when Samuel asks him to accompany him it's like him becoming Joel's father again. It's like putting your feet in a bowl of warm water when you're cold. Your whole body glows with warmth.

'Are you coming or aren't you?' asks his dad.

Joel nods. He's coming.

As they walk through the streets in the wintry darkness Joel thinks how odd it is that somebody has died in the forest that day of all days. The very day he'd decided to get lost in the forest on purpose and freeze to death in a

181

snowdrift.

He walks close to his dad. It's ages since he last did that.

'Are you sad?' asks Joel.

'Yes,' replies his father. 'It's so hard to grasp that Evert is no longer with us. It's so hard when death strikes like this. And he was only twenty-four. No more than twice your age. He said only the other day that he'd soon have saved up enough money for a motorbike. He was so proud of that. And now he's gone ...'

'What happens when you die?' asks Joel.

'If only I knew,' says his dad. 'But I don't.'

Joel doesn't know who Evert was. He's only met one of his father's workmates, and his name is Nilson but everybody calls him The Wizard. He's short and fat and speaks a funny dialect. He came back home with Samuel once, for coffee. Joel heard them talking about clubbing together to buy a rowing boat so that they could go fishing, but they got no further than talking about it. Joel heard nothing more about a boat.

He still can't grasp that he's on his way to Sara's with his dad. What he finds hardest to understand is that it's making him feel happy. First of all he's so desperate, he runs in the middle of the night to throw a stone through her window, and the next evening he's on his way to visit her with his father. He still doesn't like her. That hasn't changed. But he's going even so.

Grown-ups are not like children, he thinks. They don't understand that you can do things even if you don't want to. They don't understand that a mum who's vanished can never be replaced by somebody who wears a red hat and works as a waitress in a bar.

As they enter the rear courtyard where Sara lives, Joel feels uneasy again. What if his father suddenly stops, grabs him by the back of his neck and asks if it was Joel who threw that stone after all?

A horrible thought strikes him. What if his father has invited Joel to accompany him so that he can unmask him in front of Sara?

He stops dead.

His father turns to look at him.

'What's the matter?' he asks. 'Have you changed your mind?'

Joel tries to tell from his father's voice if his suspicion might be true. Just how much does his dad know?

'We can't stand around here,' says Samuel. 'Come on now, Joel.'

Joel sets off again, but he still feels a bit uneasy.

They walk up some dimly lit stairs.

Sara opens the door even before Samuel has knocked.

She's expecting him, Joel thinks. But she doesn't know I'm with him.

'Joel,' she says with a laugh. 'How lovely that you've come as well!'

Against his will Joel immediately takes to Sara's flat. It's not big, smaller than the one they live in, but it's light and warm, and it smells nice. Besides, she has an electric cooker.

He decides to pull his head away if she tries to pat him on the cheek, but when she does he doesn't flinch. Doesn't move at all.

The hardest thing is looking at the

broken windowpane without giving himself away.

The hole made by the stone has been covered by a piece of cardboard. The cracks go right up to the frame.

He looks at it furtively while pretending to examine a calendar hanging on the wall.

It's good that he has his back turned to Sara and his dad. They're talking about the glazier, who can't come to mend it until tomorrow. Let's hope they don't talk too long, he thinks. It could look suspicious if he spends too long examining a calendar. But then his father starts talking about the death of Evert, and Sara says she'd heard about it in the bar and it's awful.

It's not dangerous for Joel to turn round now. He sits down on a chair and listens to the conversation.

He notices that Sara has tears in her eyes. He hears her saying that she knew Evert. He'd sometimes been in the bar for a beer, but he'd never caused any trouble or had too much to drink.

Joel finds himself feeling sad as well.

He's not sure if it's because of Evert or because Sara has tears in her eyes. He can't sit here and be the only one who isn't sad.

It could have been me, he would like to say. If I hadn't been to Four Winds Lake I'd probably have frozen to death in a snowdrift. But he doesn't say it, of course. He just sits there quietly, thinking that Sara is so grown up but even so she has little tears in her eyes . . .

They keep talking about Evert for ages. Sara gives Samuel a beer and Joel a glass of juice. Then she starts making something to eat.

'Joel thinks we ought to get an electric cooker,' says Samuel all of a sudden.

'But of course you must have an electric cooker,' says Sara. 'That's obvious, surely?'

Joel likes Sara a bit more on the spot. But his father ought to have bought a cooker without her having to say anything about it.

When Sara serves the food Joel realises that he's hungry. He eats and listens. Soon he'll know all there is to know about Evert. Evert who is lying in the mortuary and never got to see Four Winds Lake ...

Joel is sitting next to his dad on a kitchen bench very similar to the one they have at home.

When they've finished eating, he feels how tired he is. How will he manage to find the strength to go out and meet Ture? What he really ought to do is have a good night's sleep and be able to go to school tomorrow without the risk of dozing off at his desk.

His father notices that Joel is tired.

'We'll go back home soon,' he says.

That makes Joel feel even more tired. He knows now that his dad will be sleeping in his own bed tonight.

When Sara suggests that he might like to have a lie down on the sofa in the other room, the one he'd thrown the stone into, he just nods and follows her. He's too tired to do anything else. More tired than he's ever been before. Besides, if he's in there his dad can't get undressed and show Sara his scar.

He can lie down in that room and keep guard.

Sara tucks him up under a blanket. Not in an offhand fashion, as if she were in a hurry to get back to the kitchen and his father. She tucks him in as if she really did want to do it properly.

'You're a nice boy,' she says. 'Your dad can be proud of you.'

Joel lies there listening to the conversation in the kitchen. They're still talking about Evert.

We'll be going home soon, he thinks. Soon . . .

When he wakes up he has no idea where he is. Then he sees that his dad is lying beside him on the sofa, fast asleep. But he's not naked, he's in his underclothes, his long johns and a vest that looks like a fishing net. Somebody must have undressed Joel as well. And put him in a flannel nightshirt . . .

He sits up slowly, being careful not to wake his father. Sara is in her own bed, her head next to the wall.

They didn't want to wake me up, he thinks. He lies down again. He has one of his dad's arms under his head.

They didn't want to wake me up. That's the only reason we're still here. But for that we'd have been at home now.

Suddenly he is wide awake. Ture will be waiting for him by the goods wagons!

He sees his dad's watch on a chair. The hands are luminous. He takes a close look, being careful not to wake Samuel: a quarter to two. Ture will have been waiting in vain.

Joel feels his stomach turn over. What will he be able to say? How will he be able to explain why he didn't turn up?

He snuggles down again, next to his dad.

Four Winds Lake, he thinks. I'll tell Ture about the trip I had with Simon Windstorm. Then he'll be bound to understand why I couldn't come.

Joel stares at the hole in the window. He thinks about the dog somewhere out there in the night.

The dog on its way to a star . . .

Who is that, playing music for him?

Joel is dreaming about the rowing boat on Four Winds Lake. Now it's no longer winter. The boat is bobbing among the little ripples and Joel is lying on the bottom, which smells of tar, and gazing up at the blue sky.

But who's that playing?

The music is coming from somewhere or other. Somebody he can't see is playing a piano made of crystal glass. The tune keeps repeating itself, over and over again, getting weaker all the time, slower . . .

He wants to stay in the boat but he finds himself rising up towards the blue sky, as if his body were being forced up by Four Winds Lake, and soon he's hovering high above the boat which he can see a long way down below . . .

Then he opens his eyes and the tune accompanies him out of the dream. On his chest, just under his chin, is a musical box. Sara has put it there. A little man made of wood is clashing two cymbals. He's standing on the lid of the red musical box.

Joel watches the little wooden man's arms moving more and more slowly, just as the tune is fading away . . .

Sara is standing in the kitchen doorway, smiling at him. She's wearing her working clothes, the black skirt and white blouse.

'Time to get up,' she says.

'Where's Samuel?' asks Joel.

But he doesn't need to ask. His father has already been working in the forest for several hours. Sawing and chopping while the snow-covered trees stand all round him, waiting to be felled.

'You were fast asleep,' says Sara. 'He didn't want to wake you up last night. You were sleeping like a log.'

Logs don't sleep, he thinks. Logs don't breathe, don't laugh, don't sleep. A log can't think, can't speak. A log is just a log . . .

He tumbles out of bed and gets dressed. There is a bowl of porridge waiting for him in the kitchen.

It feels odd, not having to make my

191

own breakfast, he thinks as he eats.

Sara is standing in front of a wall mirror, combing her hair. She fixes it behind her ears with two hairpins.

He notices that her ears stick out slightly. Not a lot, but it's noticeable. And she makes no effort to hide the fact.

'That was a terrific alarm clock,' he says.

As he leaves she pats him on the cheek.

'You'll have to hurry up now,' she says. 'It's late.'

He takes the short cut through the churchyard, but doesn't jump over Nils Wiberg's family grave.

He decides to say that he's had a bad cold when Miss Nederström asks him why he hasn't been at school. If he snorts through his nose before entering the classroom, it will get blocked up. Then Miss Nederström will be able to hear that he's had a cold.

He decides that he's had a temperature of 38.6 degrees. In order to be believed, he must avoid sounding vague. Not 38 degrees, but 38.6.

To his surprise, however, she doesn't ask and the school day passes without anything unusual happening.

Otto has fallen ill again, and Joel hopes that he's going to be off school so long that he has to repeat the year again next year. It's a nasty thought, but Joel doesn't care if Otto has to spend the rest of his life repeating the year.

On the way home he calls in at the grocer's. Svenson is sitting on a chair behind the counter and has a headache.

'Potatoes,' says Joel. 'And milk. A box of matches. And a jar of pickled herring.'

Svenson groans as he stands up. He blinks hard at Joel, as if he were finding it hard to stay awake.

'Tell your dad he'd better come in and pay his bills pretty soon now,' he says. 'It's a month since he last paid.'

Joel promises to pass on the message, but he reckons Svenson can wait for another month. The first priority is buying an electric cooker, and then The Flying Horse. His dad won't have enough money for much more than that.

When he gets home he sits down at the kitchen table and writes up his logbook.

He writes about Simon Windstorm and Four Winds Lake. Simon Windstorm has just been released after being captured and held a prisoner for ten years by natives in Sumatra. They go for a walk together round the shore of the remarkable island called Four Winds Island . . .

Then he sits on the window seat in the hall, waiting for his father to come home.

It's been thawing. The sun has already gone down, but melted snow is still dripping down from the roof.

He's worried about seeing Ture later tonight. He hopes Ture won't turn up. He'd prefer to be on his own, looking for the dog, always assuming he goes out at all.

Joel thinks about his Secret Society. It hasn't turned out as he'd envisaged. There again, he's not really sure what he had in mind when he first started it all. The only thing that is absolutely sure is the dog. The dog that ran down the street in the middle of the night, and looked round, as if it were frightened of something. That's where it all started.

I must find that dog, Joel thinks.

It's important. Why it's important, I don't know. But what I do know is that I have to find it before it vanishes when it reaches its star . . .

He doesn't know why he thinks it's going to run off into space. Possibly because it sounds fascinating? Possibly because it can be a sort of password? Or a magic spell?

Why do you sometimes have thoughts you don't understand? he wonders.

As if there was somebody else inside your head, choosing thoughts for you.

He breathes onto the windowpane and writes his name in the mist.

Joel isn't a bad name. Otto is a bad name. Joel is good because it's not all that common, but not too uncommon either. There's only one other boy at his school called Joel, but there are definitely ten called Tore and maybe as many as twenty called Margareta.

Joel thinks up two rules. He jumps down from the window seat and takes his logbook out of *Celestine*'s glass case.

Rules for Joel Gustafson, he writes. Rules that must always be obeyed.

You don't need to be best, but you must never be worst, he writes. That's rule number one.

If you think something is bad you must look for something that is worse, he writes. When you find something that's worse, whatever it was that felt bad won't seem quite so bad any longer. That's rule number two.

He thinks that the rules are a bit long, but he can't think of a shorter way of expressing them. Sometimes it seems as if there aren't enough words.

He hears the front door close with a bang down below, then his father's footsteps coming up the stairs.

Joel has forgotten all about the potatoes. He stuffs the logbook into his pocket and starts putting firewood in the stove. His father is coughing and clearing his throat in the hall as he takes off his jacket.

'I think I'm getting a cold,' he says as he comes into the kitchen and sits down on a chair. Joel helps him off with his boots. Samuel smells very strongly of sweat today.

'Phew, what a stink!' he says, pulling a face. 'We'd better gather together all our dirty linen tonight.'

Joel's dad has an old, worn-out sailor's kitbag that they use for dirty washing. When it's full he takes it to a widow called Mrs Nilson who launders it. She lives in the same building as Svenson's grocery shop.

After dinner Samuel brings out the big zinc bath. Joel boils some water on the stove, and has to go downstairs twice for more firewood.

His dad settles into the bath with his knees up under his chin. Joel always has to laugh whenever he sees him hunched up like this, barely able to move.

'What's so funny?' asks Samuel.

'Nothing,' says Joel.

Then he gives his dad's back a good scrubbing.

'Scrub harder,' says Samuel. 'I think I've got bark all over my skin after chopping down so many damned trees. Scrub harder . . .'

Then it's Joel's turn. His dad gives him a good scrubbing as well, and cuts his nails. Then they sit in front of the stove to dry out, wrapped up in towels.

'This is something we won't be able to do when we have an electric cooker,' says Samuel. 'Maybe we could crawl into the oven to dry instead.'

Then he becomes serious.

'I'm going to see Evert's mother tonight,' he says. 'I have to pass on my condolences.'

When they've finished drying themselves, Samuel takes his black suit out of the wardrobe. He's hardly ever worn it. They both examine it closely under the kitchen light, making sure there is no sign of any moth-holes.

'I bought this suit in England,' says Joel's dad. 'In a place called Middlesbrough. I bought it off a Chinaman who came on board our ship while we were in port. I thought it was too expensive, but it's worn well.'

He shows Joel a label sewn into the jacket's inside pocket.

'There you see,' he says. 'Made in England. Your dad doesn't get dressed up in any old rubbish.'

Joel has to help fasten his dad's tie. He gets it wrong over and over again until he remembers exactly how to tie the knot. His father is puffing and complaining because his shirt is too tight.

'The suit's fine,' he says. 'It comes from England. But this shirt is some botched job by a useless tailor in Västergötland. It's much too tight.'

'Maybe it's the wrong size,' says Joel.

'Size and size,' says his dad. 'A shirt ought to fit, that's all there is to it.'

Then he dips his comb into some water and combs his unruly hair. Joel holds the shaving mirror so that his dad can check the back of his head.

'Do I look all right?' he asks eventually.

Joel walks round, inspecting him. He's not used to seeing his father dressed up. He wonders how many other boys have dads with a suit bought in England.

'I was wearing this suit when we got married,' says Samuel. 'Jenny, your mother, and me. I could have shown you, but she took the wedding photo with her.'

'Why do you never tell me about her?' asks Joel.

'I will do,' says his dad. 'But not just now. I have to go.'

'Will you be coming back home?' asks Joel.

'Of course I'll be coming back home,' says his father. 'I shan't be long. But she's sitting all on her own now, Evert's mum, crying her eyes out. We're all going to see her, all of us who used to work with him. Bosses from the forestry company have already been. Obviously, we have to go and visit her. Evert's dad didn't have to see his son die. He passed away a few years ago.'

He falls silent. Joel helps him on with his boots.

'Wave, won't you?' shouts Joel as his

dad goes down the stairs.

When he emerges into the street, Samuel pauses and looks up at the window where Joel is perched. They wave to each other, then Samuel walks off down the street.

Joel carefully lifts *Celestine* out of her glass case and blows the dust away from her sails and the railings. He finds a dead fly in one of the holds. When he pokes it out with a match stalk, one of its wings falls off. The fly makes him think of Evert.

He doesn't want to. Not now. He shudders at the thought that he'd planned to go and lie down in a snowdrift and freeze to death.

He banishes the thought and puts *Celestine* back in her case. Then he picks out one of his dad's rolled-up sea charts and spreads it out on the kitchen table. He reads all the names and the depth soundings, and works out suitable routes for the ship he is captain of.

All this exists, he thinks. All this is lying in store for me. If Dad doesn't want to come with me, I'll go there myself one of these days . . .

He rolls up the chart and returns it to its place. Then he snuggles down in bed and carries on dreaming about the sea that's waiting for him out there . . .

He wakes up when his dad comes back home.

'How did it go?' he asks when Samuel looks in on him.

'Are you awake? I thought you were asleep.'

He comes in and sits on Joel's bed.

'It wasn't a very pleasant experience,' he says.

Joel sits up in bed and helps his father off with his tie. Samuel suddenly gives him a big hug.

'Go to sleep now,' he says.

Joel can see that his eyes are red. He leaves the room and before long, Joel hears him gargling in the kitchen. The radio is on at very low volume in his father's room. The bed creaks, and then the radio goes quiet.

Joel puts the alarm clock under his pillow. Then he goes back to sea in his thoughts, stands on the bridge and feels a warm breeze caressing his cheeks . . .

*   *   *

He woke up at midnight and got dressed, and now he's waiting for Ture in the shadow of a goods wagon.

His ears are skinned—he doesn't want Ture to creep up on him again without him hearing.

He turns round and tries to penetrate the darkness. He can hear an engine in the distance and wonders if it's The Old Bricklayer driving round in his lorry.

All of a sudden he finds Ture standing by his side. He's done it again.

'Where were you last night?' asks Ture.

Joel explains what happened. It's too dark for him to see if Ture believes him or not.

'Let's go,' says Ture when Joel has finished.

Joel follows him down to the bridge.

Ture stops under the enormous

203

arches and suddenly produces a pair of shears he'd had hidden under his jacket.

'Now it's your turn,' he says. 'Last night I did what we'd agreed to do. I smeared her currant bushes with varnish. It's your turn tonight. You're going to cut the plants she has climbing up her walls with these shears.'

'We hadn't agreed to do anything,' says Joel. 'I didn't want to smear varnish over her currant bushes And I don't intend to cut back any of her plants.'

'Just as I thought,' says Ture. 'You're a coward.'

'I'm not a coward.'

'You daren't do it.'

'I do. But I don't want to.'

Ture looks scornfully at him.

'If you betray The Secret Society, you have to crawl over the arch,' he says, spitting. 'Well, you've betrayed it. You didn't turn up last night. I waited but you never appeared. In a Secret Society you don't come out with a series of excuses. You do what you've agreed to do.'

Ture gazes up at the high arches.

'Well, I'm waiting,' he says with a smirk.

The penny drops. Ture wants him to climb over one of the arches.

'I couldn't come last night,' he says. 'That's all there is to it.'

He wishes he'd said that in a firm voice. Instead of speaking so softly and hesitantly.

Ture holds out the pair of shears.

'It's the climbing plants or the bridge,' he says.

'But I've told you, I couldn't come!'

It sounded as if he were almost squeaking. A scared little baby bird that hardly dares to open its beak.

Joel tries to think. It's hard to think clearly when you have to think quickly. He knows that, but he hasn't yet learnt how to do it.

'I need a pee,' he says to gain time.

He takes a few strides to one side and turns his back on Ture.

'You could have a piss from the top of the bridge,' says Ture, and Joel can tell that he's smirking.

205

Joel unzips his flies and tries to produce a few drops while he thinks.

He doesn't want to clip any climbing plants. He doesn't want to climb over the arch either.

Why should Ture force him to choose between doing something that's wicked and something else that's also bad? He hasn't betrayed The Secret Society. There's no rule that says you mustn't oversleep.

Ture uses so many words, he thinks. He can talk till the cows come home. Joel feels angry.

He doesn't want to tip ants in through open windows and he doesn't want to smear currant bushes with varnish.

He wants to look for the dog.

He doesn't want to do anything he doesn't want to do.

Even so, he grabs hold of the shears.

'I'll do it,' he says. 'But not because I've betrayed The Secret Society.'

They cross over the bridge and turn into No-Nose's street. They stop outside her gate.

'I'll wait here,' says Ture.

206

'You can wait wherever you like,' says Joel.

He opens the gate slowly. The house is in darkness. Even so, he has the feeling that it's watching him. Like a bird of prey waiting to pounce on him.

Cautiously, he moves closer. When he turns round, there is no sign of Ture. He's hidden himself in the shadows.

In front of him is the wall and the climbing plants. In winter there are only bare branches spreading all over the wall like a big spider's web, but in summer the whole wall is covered in green leaves.

He listens again.

He carefully inserts the shears between the wall and the branches, and clips.

And again. And again.

A door opens and a light goes on. He's bathed in light and his heart starts pounding.

No-Nose Gertrud is standing in the doorway, looking at him. The black hole that ought to be a nose is gaping wide. He notices that she is barefoot.

'What do you think you're doing?' she says.

It doesn't occur to Joel to run away.

She doesn't sound angry at all, he thinks. Not frightened either. Just sad.

'Come here,' she says.

Joel glances at the gate, but Ture is nowhere to be seen. He knows he ought to run away. She wouldn't be able to catch up with him.

But he stays where he is even so.

'Come here,' she says again.

If only she'd sounded angry, thinks Joel. Then I could have run away. But how can you run away from somebody who just sounds sad?

He goes up to the door.

'Come into the kitchen where we can talk,' she says. 'It's so cold out here. I'm freezing.'

Joel knows he shouldn't go inside with her. He'll be trapped if he does. But he can't help but go in anyway.

It's warm in her kitchen. He's standing in the middle of the floor and doesn't know what to do with the pair of shears.

She leaves the room. When she

comes back he sees she's stuffed a handkerchief into the hole under her eyes.

The dirty snow is dripping off Joel's boots. He tries to stand in such a way that she can't see the pool. No-Nose is wearing a black coat, and he can see that she only has a nightgown underneath.

'Who are you?' she asks.

Joel doesn't answer.

I can invent a name, he thinks. Or I can say I'm called Otto.

'I'm not going to hit you,' she says. 'Even though I'm very strong. I just want to know why you're doing this. One morning I find my kitchen full of ants. The next morning I discover that somebody has killed my currant bushes. They'll never have any berries again. And now you are clipping off my climbing plants.

Create fear, Joel thinks. That's what Ture said.

Create sorrow is what he ought to have said.

And where is Ture now? He ought to have come to rescue Joel. If any member of The Secret Society is captured, other members have to help to set him free, of course. You don't need to make a rule about that.

Joel doesn't know what to say. He stares down at the floor and tries to hide the shears behind his back.

'Why?' she asks again.

'I want to go home now,' says Joel.

That is the only thing he can think of to say that is absolutely true. Without warning she leaves the kitchen again. A gramophone starts playing, and when she reappears she's carrying a trombone. She stands in front of him and starts playing, the same tune as on the gramophone. She's stuffed a scarf into the bell of the trombone, to muffle the sound. She sways in time to the music, and Joel thinks she plays well—it sounds as if the trombone is part of the gramophone record.

Then the needle gets stuck. There's a crackling noise and the same notes are repeated over and over again.

Gertrud does the same thing with her trombone. She's watching him all the time. The same notes, over and over again. Then she stamps on the floor, the needle rights itself and the record plays to the end.

Afterwards, when everything is quiet, the sound of the trombone is still echoing in Joel's ears.

'Why do you think I played?' she asks.

Joel shakes his head. He doesn't know.

'Just because you're deformed, it doesn't mean you're an idiot,' she says. 'Even if you don't have a nose you can learn how to blow and make the trombone sing. If I'd still had a nose I don't suppose I'd ever have learnt how to play the trombone . . .'

Then she smiles at him.

'Do you understand what I mean?' she asks.

Joel shakes his head again. No, he doesn't follow.

'I like redcurrants and blackcurrants,' she says. 'I like to have leaves climbing up my wall in summer. I like ants as well, but not when I find them in my kitchen in winter.'

She puts the trombone down on the

table.

Joel tries to imagine what it looked like when the kitchen was full of ants.

'I know what people whisper about me,' she says. 'I know a lot of people think I shouldn't be allowed to walk around in the street like other folk. Perhaps they think I ought to be shut up in a cage and put on show as a freak? For ten years I couldn't bear to look at myself in a mirror. Now I can. And I want my currant bushes leaving in peace.'

It's easier now, thinks Joel, now that she sounds angry. You can understand that.

'What's your name?' she asks.

'Joel Gustafson,' he says.

He regrets mentioning his surname the moment he's said it. It would have been enough just to say Joel.

'Why did you do all this?'

How can you explain something you can't explain? he wonders. Besides, it was Ture who said they must create fear. Ture, who's no longer there. Ture, who hid in the shadows and allowed Joel to be the only one who was caught.

'I want to know,' she says.

She grabs hold of him by the shoulders and gives him a good shake. He can feel that she's strong. Her face is very close to his.

He can't help but stare at the handkerchief stuffed into her nose. She shakes him very hard. Then she drops her hands.

'Go now,' she says. 'But come back and tell me why you did it once you've understood why yourself.'

She looks at him, with sadness in her eyes.

'Don't promise me to come,' she says. 'Promise yourself. Go now ...'

She shuts the door behind him.

As he goes out through the gate he can hear that she's started playing the trombone again.

He looks round for Ture. No sign.

He can still hear the sound of the trombone coming through the house walls. He wishes he'd told her the facts. At the same time, he's relieved that she let him go.

He runs down the street to the

bridge. It's still thawing, and he slips and almost falls.

As he crosses the bridge Ture suddenly emerges from the shadows.

'I didn't expect that,' he says. 'That you'd get caught.'

Joel is furious now.

He hurls the shears down at Ture's feet.

'I'm glad you'll soon be running away,' he says.

Ture eyes him scornfully.

'Before I run away I'll make sure you climb over that arch,' he says. 'You got caught before you did what you'd promised to do.'

'I'll climb over the bridge tomorrow night,' says Joel. 'I'll stand on the top and pee all over you.'

Then he runs off. He can hear Ture laughing behind him.

I shall climb over that arch, he thinks indignantly. I shall climb up and stand at the very top and pee all over his head. The Secret Society is mine, not his.

My task is to find a dog heading for a distant star. Not creating fear in people who in fact only feel sorrow.

Ture is so odd, he thinks. He uses so many words. You can never be sure what he's thinking. He's not like the rest of us. No doubt he's rich. He doesn't go to school . . .

As he turns a corner The Old Bricklayer comes driving past in his lorry. Joel stops and waves, but The Old Bricklayer doesn't see him. Joel watches the red rear lights gleaming like animals' eyes in the darkness.

Adventure, he thinks. This is where it's to be found! Simon Windstorm, No-Nose, Four Winds Lake . . .

And the dog.

The dog running and running inside his head . . .

Samuel is snoring away in his room. Joel gets undressed and creeps into bed.

Is he dreaming about the sea? Joel wonders. Dreaming about Jenny or Sara? Or is he dreaming about me?

He looks at the hands of his alarm clock glowing in the darkness.

Twenty-four hours from now he'll have climbed over the iron bridge.

Scrambled up one side of the arch, stood up on top, unzipped his fly, and then scrambled down the other side.

He'll show Ture von Swallow how you conquer a bridge. Then Ture can run away if he wants, but he'll never be able to claim that Joel Gustafson is a coward.

What was it he'd thought the first time he saw Ture on the rock by the river?

That he was an unpleasant, smirking stranger? Somebody who made him angry on sight? Well, now Joel will show him. Joel will sort him . . .

He checks his alarm clock. Nearly two.

Climbing over the bridge arch is dangerous, he thinks. It's not allowed because it's dangerous.

He suddenly feels scared. What has he let himself in for?

Can he think up something else to do, so that he doesn't need to climb? The only thing would be to take the shears and cut back the rest of the plants growing up No-Nose's wall.

But he can't do that. He would never

be able to survive seeing her open the door again and stand barefoot on the cold steps.

Exhaustion is rolling over him in waves.

It's a long time to tomorrow, he thinks. So many seconds that he can't possibly count them all.

He's on the point of falling asleep when he hears No-Nose's trombone again. He can see her swaying in time to the music as she plays. All those repeated notes, over and over again.

He remembers what she said: Don't promise me, promise yourself.

I must write up everything that happens in the logbook, he thinks. I promise to do that. I promise myself not to forget.

The following day Joel falls asleep at his desk again, but he wakes up so quickly that Miss Nederström doesn't notice. His eyelids are so heavy that he has to sit with his head in his hands, and hold them up with his fingers.

After school he hurries home. He lies down on the bed and sets the alarm clock. He can snatch an hour's sleep before he needs to start lighting the stove.

He's very tired, but he can't sleep. He imagines himself staring up at the iron railway bridge. It gets higher and higher even as he watches. In the end it looks to him as if the top of the arches disappear into the clouds.

He sits up in bed.

He knows he can't do it.

If he falls off the bridge, he'll die. Just like Evert did when the tree hit him.

But what can he do?

The only thing he can think of is not to go out tonight. Not to go out at all until Ture has run away.

But what had Ture said? That he wasn't going to go away until Joel had climbed over the bridge?

His thoughts are buzzing around in his head. Is it really all that dangerous, climbing over the bridge arch? Provided he holds on tightly and doesn't look down? He's good at climbing trees, after all. He never falls, never gets dizzy.

Of course I dare do it, he tells

himself, and discards the frightened thoughts. It's the thoughts that are scared. Not me . . .

When his dad comes home the potatoes are ready.

Samuel has a cold. He's coughing and shivering and thinks he has a temperature. He goes to bed as soon as he's finished eating. Joel takes him a cup of coffee.

Samuel suddenly starts talking.

'Joel,' he says. 'As soon as you leave school we'll go away from here. We'll move to somewhere with a harbour. I can't stand these forests any longer. I want to see the open sea. As soon as you leave school, we'll move.'

Three more years, Joel thinks. Only three more years!

Joel jumps up on the bed and sits astride his father.

'Is that definite?' he says. 'Absolutely definite?'

His father nods. Yes, it is.

'But you're too heavy to be sitting on me like this,' he says.

Joel moves and sits on the edge of the bed.

He has so many questions.

Which sea? Which town? Only three more years . . .

'I think I must get some sleep,' says his father. 'I feel as if I've got a temperature.'

He closes his eyes, and Joel goes to sit in the window. One year, two years, three years. He tries to work out how he can make those three years pass as quickly as possible.

The summers always pass quickly. So do the springs. It's the autumns and winters that are so long. Especially the winters, that never seem to end. Time always passes more quickly after Christmas than before.

He realises that the three years will pass very slowly. There's nothing he can do about that.

Then he starts thinking about the railway bridge. It's out there in the darkness, waiting for him.

The scared thoughts come creeping up on him again, but he sends them packing. I'll show that Ture, he thinks. I'll show him all right . . .

His father is fast asleep when he

tiptoes out into the darkness, shortly before midnight.

It's grown colder again. The snow under his feet is frozen. The sky is clear and full of stars, and the new moon hovers over the wooded hills. He pauses to look at The Plough. It's the only constellation whose name he knows.

In the southern sky is a constellation called The Southern Cross. His dad's told him about it. Sailors used to navigate by that constellation a long time ago. You can stand on deck and look at The Southern Cross. In the middle of the night when a warm breeze is blowing.

He finds that hard to imagine. Standing to look at stars without it being cold.

He approaches the bridge.

If Ture is waiting by the goods wagons, he can carry on waiting there until it dawns on him that Joel has gone straight to the bridge.

He stares up at the arches and tries to make them shrink by looking at them. They are not so high, not so narrow as they seem.

It will take three minutes to creep over an arch.

Maybe five.

Five minutes isn't very long.

It's such a short part of your life that you don't even notice it.

Now he can see Ture running towards him from the direction of the marshalling yard.

Joel suddenly finds it hard to keep his fear at bay again. He sees that Ture has the pair of shears with him.

That makes him angry, and when he gets angry his fear starts to go away. It doesn't vanish altogether, but it grows smaller.

'You could have left the shears at home,' he says. 'Stand in the middle of the bridge and I'll pee all over your head.'

Ture smirks.

'You'll never climb over the arch,' he says. 'You'll slither back down again.'

'We'll see about that,' says Joel. 'Go and stand in the middle.'

Ture shrugs and heads for the middle of the bridge.

Now Joel is alone with the bridge.

It's bigger than ever now.

Joel stands by the abutment and gazes up at one of the arches soaring up into the darkness. Underneath is the frozen river.

OK, it's just a matter of climbing. Not thinking. Not looking down.

He clambers up onto the parapet, next to where the arch begins. If he stretches both arms out he can just reach far enough to cling onto the sides.

That's what he must do. Press up against the centre of the arch, hold on tightly to the two sides, and slowly ease his way upwards.

He lays his hand on the iron. The cold immediately penetrates his glove. He closes his eyes and starts edging upwards.

Like a frog, he thinks. Like a frog trying to get away from a beast of prey that's just behind him.

The iron rivets are scraping against his knees.

First he moves one hand, then the opposite leg. Then the other hand and the other leg. Slowly, slowly . . .

He's surrounded by silence.

He closes his eyes and keeps edging upwards. One hand, the opposite leg.

The iron is extremely cold and already he feels frozen to death. Every time he eases himself upwards it becomes harder to keep his fear at bay.

Why am I doing this? he asks himself in desperation. I'll never do it. I'll fall down and kill myself . . .

Then he hears Ture shouting to him.

Only then does he realise how high up he is. Ture's voice sounds so far away.

'Come down,' he shouts. 'Come down . . .'

Why should he go down? Is Ture so afraid that he'll succeed?

He keeps on edging upwards like a terrified frog. The rivets are digging into his skin and he can feel that his arms are starting to go to sleep.

Oh, Dad, he thinks. I'm not going to make it. You'll have to come and help me . . .

He notices that the arch is beginning to level out.

Then he comes to the very top. Now he'll have to start going downwards. Now he'll have to climb headfirst.

Panic strikes.

He can't keep going.

He clings on with all his strength. He can't move. Neither forwards nor backwards.

It suddenly feels warm down one of his legs. He doesn't know why.

He shouts out, just once, a piercing shriek into the darkness ...

He has no idea what's happening down below.

He thinks he can hear The Old Bricklayer's lorry. Or is it No-Nose's trombone, perhaps?

Otto is standing there, laughing. Miss Nederström is there as well, and she's angry. The whole bridge is full of people laughing. The whole school are down below on the bridge, pointing and laughing ...

He can also hear his father's voice.

But his dad isn't laughing. He's shouting something, but Joel can't hear what it is because the voice is coming from so far away.

The voice is slowly getting nearer.

Now he can hear that his father is quite close.

'Lie completely still. Don't move at all, Joel. Don't move ...'

Why is he saying that?

Joel is incapable of moving. He'll have to lie here at the top of the arch for the next thousand years ...

Now his father's voice is right behind him.

'Don't move,' he whispers. 'Lie completely still ...'

Then something happens that he'll never forget, for as long as he lives.

His dad takes hold of Joel's back, so tenderly.

He can't see a thing because his face is pressed up against the cold arch. But even so, he knows it's his father's hand. There's only one hand like that in the whole wide world.

He feels the hand and hears his father's voice behind him.

'Creep backwards. Slowly. I'll hold on to you ...'

Joel starts to return slowly to the ground.

He's no longer clinging on to the axis of the earth. He's going slowly back to the ground.

He edges slowly down with his numb arms and legs.

All the time his dad is whispering reassuringly to him.

At last he feels the bridge parapet against his foot.

His dad lifts him down and hugs him tight. Then he's lifted into the cab of a lorry and it's The Old Bricklayer sitting behind the wheel.

Ture is hanging around outside. Joel can see that his face is different. Ture is scared.

His father carries him up the stairs. Mrs Westman is watching from her doorway. He hears his dad telling her about an accident that didn't happen.

Then he's in his own bed and Samuel is rubbing his feet.

He drinks something hot, and then all he wants to do is sleep . . .

But before he goes to sleep he wants his dad to tell him about the sea.

About breakers and dolphins, and the warm monsoon winds that come from India . . .

It still feels as if he's clinging on to the cold iron arch.

His dad tells him about the warm monsoon winds, and only then can he start to loosen his grip on the freezing cold arch.

Then everything becomes a dream.

Celestine grows out of her case and turns into a big sailing ship bobbing in the swell as the sun starts to set. She's waiting for a wind to blow. Joel is in his hammock below deck. Swaying slowly from side to side, deeper and deeper into slumber . . .

8

The following day Joel found out what had happened.

When he woke up his dad was sitting on his bed, and through the door he could see Mrs Westman busy with a saucepan in the kitchen. Even before his dad rolled up the blinds Joel knew that spring was on the way at last.

He could tell from the birds chirruping outside the window.

He no longer felt cold when he woke up, but his knees were sore and when he felt under the covers he found he had scabs on both his legs.

Samuel hadn't gone to work in the forest that day. He'd stayed at home, sat on Joel's bed and talked to him.

It was Ture who had realised that Joel would never be able to get down from the arch. He'd run towards the streetlights and before long Simon Windstorm had come trundling up in his lorry. Ture had stood in the middle of the road, waving with both hands. Simon Windstorm had barely been able to understand what Ture said, partly because he was so agitated and out of breath, and partly because of his odd dialect.

But Simon had understood enough to grasp that an accident had taken place, or perhaps was about to take place.

They'd driven to the railway bridge and he'd seen what looked like a bundle of clothes clinging on to the top of the arch. When he asked who it was up there, Ture said it was Joel Gustafson, and Simon gathered it was the boy who had been with him to Four Winds Lake. He'd left Ture on the railway bridge in case anything were to happen, then driven to the house where he'd dropped Joel a few days previously.

As he didn't know which was Joel's door, he'd knocked on all of them. Old Mrs Westman had been scared to death and hardly dared to open up. She'd just peeped out hesitantly through a narrow crack. Samuel had answered the door, full of cold and with a temperature. When he heard that Joel was stuck on top of one of the arches on the railway bridge, he'd barely paused to get dressed. He'd pulled on his trousers over his pyjamas, and forgotten to put a sock on one foot. Joel could remember the rest, more or less, himself.

His dad had climbed up behind him and helped him down. Then Simon Windstorm had driven them home in his lorry.

Now it was morning.

Mrs Westman had knocked on the door as early as five o'clock to see if she could help them with anything. She'd lit the stove, and sighed and tutted at the terrible accident that had very nearly taken place.

But Joel was asleep.

He'd shouted out in his sleep several times, as if he'd been climbing up the arch again.

His dad carried the worn-out old armchair into Joel's room and stayed there all night, wrapped in a blanket.

Simon Windstorm had stayed for a coffee, but as Joel was asleep and it was clear that he didn't seem to be ill, he'd driven home in his lorry. That was at about four o'clock.

Before leaving he'd told Samuel that he and Joel had been to the little lake they called Four Winds Lake. He also told Samuel some of the things Joel had told him about.

They had no idea where Ture had disappeared to, with his shears. They didn't even know who he was.

But why had he been on the bridge in

the middle of the night with a pair of shears? There are a lot of things that Samuel wants to ask Joel about, but he decides to wait a bit. Just now the most important thing is for Joel to understand that he's not still stuck on the top of that arch. He has to grasp that it's only a memory. Something that's over and done with. Something he might not be able to forget. Nor should forget. But it's in the past now.

Joel listens to what his father has to say.

But even as he does so, he's thinking about something entirely different. He's thinking about the dog he saw that night.

The dog that had stopped, sniffed the air and looked all around, as if it were scared of something.

Without knowing why, Joel suspects everything that's happened has to do with that dog.

He has to find the dog.

Maybe his dad could help him to look for it if he explains how important it is for him to find it?

His knees hurt and he'd rather not

think about what had happened during the night.

It's something important that he can't understand.

What happened up there when the arch flattened out at the top? What happened when he was beaten by the bridge?

'A penny for your thoughts,' says his dad.

Joel shakes his head.

'I'm not thinking about anything,' he says.

That's a silly answer. Nobody can think about nothing. But he doesn't want to share the thoughts that are buzzing around in his mind with anybody.

His dad looks tired.

Joel wonders why he isn't angry. He ought to be. Joel could have fallen off the arch and killed himself.

'You could have killed yourself, you know,' says his dad, as if he'd been reading Joel's thoughts. 'I'd never have got over that.'

Those were his exact words.

I'd never have got over that.

At that moment Joel realises that his dad will never abandon him. He'll never do what his mum did.

Even if he does go with Sara and sleeps in her bed, he'll never run away.

Joel is absolutely certain of that now.

If he hadn't tried to climb over the arch he might never have got to know that.

It does occur to him that he ought to have realised even so.

He ought to have brushed aside the nasty thoughts. Ignored them.

In the afternoon Samuel goes to Svenson's grocery shop to buy a few things.

Mrs Westman has gone back to her embroidery. The whole house is silent.

Joel gets up and puts on his dad's dressing gown. It's so long that it trails behind him.

Who came out on top? he wonders. Was it the bridge that won, or was it me? I didn't climb over the arch, but I didn't fall off and kill myself.

Maybe nobody won. Who's the winner if nobody wins?

He fetches the logbook from under

Celestine and starts writing. 'During yesterday's violent storm Captain Samuel Gustafson climbed up a mast to rescue an injured lookout. Once again Captain Samuel Gustafson carried out yet another heroic deed . . .'

Joel reads through what he's written, and it occurs to him that he ought to go back to the railway bridge. He must establish how high up he was. He has to do that in order to work out what really happened . . .

His dad makes pancakes for dinner. He burns himself on the stove and the pancakes turn black and stick to the pan. He'd also forgotten to buy any jam.

'I made a bit of a mess of this,' he says apologetically. 'There was a time when I could make perfect pancakes on a ship at the height of a storm. Now they're all black and burnt.'

'No problem,' says Joel. 'Burnt pancakes are pretty good as well.'

When they've finished eating Joel announces that he intends to go out.

His dad frowns.

'Where are you going?'

'I'm not going to climb over the arch. I'll soon be back.'

'You ought to stay in tonight.'

But Joel was already lacing up his boots.

'I'll soon be back,' he says.

When he comes out into the street, he finds that it's still thawing. Perhaps winter is coming to an end at last.

Samuel is watching him from a window. Joel waves.

He arrives at the bridge just as the evening's last train is thundering past. It's a passenger train heading for the northern forests and whatever lies beyond. Joel stops to count the carriages. The engine puffs away as it clatters over the bridge. He watches it disappearing into the darkness.

Then he walks out onto the bridge and gazes up at the gigantic arches.

He was lying up there.

He got that far.

So far that he panicked and peed himself.

When he pictures himself up there at the top of the arch, a terrified frog

236

clinging on for dear life, he is overcome by fear.

Only now does it register what he's done.

If he'd continued he'd have been bound to lose his grip and fall onto the frozen river.

He'd have ceased to exist. It would have been as if he'd never lived.

He sees somebody walking over the bridge, and recognises Ture. Ture von Swallow with his shears.

They stand face to face, without speaking.

Then Ture holds out the shears.

'You didn't complete the climb,' he says. 'And you didn't pee on my head.'

Joel sees red.

'I can do it again,' he says.

'If I hadn't run for help, you'd still be up there,' says Ture.

Then Joel thumps him.

His fist hits Ture in the face. Ture is so surprised that he falls over backwards and drops the shears. It dawns on Joel that Ture is even worse than Otto. He can argue and fight with Otto, but all the time he knows why.

Ture is different. Ture makes it seem as if The Secret Society is his, and that Joel is a servant who has to do as he's told.

The worst thing about Ture is that it's so hard not to do what he tells you. It's so easy to think that what he says is right.

In fact it's the shears that make Joel so angry. When he sees them he realises that Ture still thinks he should cut back Gertrud's climbing plants.

Ture has got to his feet again, but the shears are still lying between the rails.

Now he'll hit me back, Joel thinks. But Ture just stares at him.

Joel can see that he's frightened, and that gives Joel the upper hand.

'You come here and claim you're something special,' he says. 'Special and stuck-up . . .'

Now he'll thump me, Joel thinks.

But Ture just keeps on staring at him. That's when Joel realises that what Ture has said about running away isn't true. He doesn't know why he is sure of that, but he's certain even so.

'You're no longer a member of my

Secret Society,' he says. 'You'll have to start a society of your own.'

It seems to Joel that Ture looks so small.

He comes here and plays the Big Man, Joel thinks. Speaks in a funny way and thinks he's somebody special just because his father's a judge and he has a room of his own with lots of fancy machines.

There are stewards on board ship. Servants. His dad has told him about them. But Joel has no intention of being Ture's steward.

'If we're going to be friends, you'll have to act like a civilised human being,' says Joel.

That's something he's heard his dad say. You can't have friends who don't act like civilised human beings. But Ture is no doubt incapable of that. He wants servants, not friends. He wants people to feel frightened by him, and then do whatever he tells them to do.

Joel walks away. He doesn't turn round to look. He's pleased with himself because he ended up on top. But at the same time he thinks of

Ture's room and all the things he could have done there. Being the only member of his Secret Society isn't very good either. But he decides that it's necessary. And perhaps Ture will change for the better?

It seems to Joel that life consists of far too many perhapses.

And there's far too little you can know for certain.

Samuel is in the window looking out for him when Joel comes home. Joel waves, then tries to reach the top of the stairs in three jumps. He nearly manages it. Soon he'll be successful.

The following day he goes to school as usual. Nobody seems to know about what happened at the bridge. Not even Otto, who's back at school again, and marches towards him over the playground with his sneering smile.

Joel realises he is the bearer of a big secret . . .

That evening, when they've finished eating, he starts getting ready to go out.

'Going out again?' asks his dad. 'What are you going to do this time?'

Joel would prefer to tell him the truth. That he's going to see if the girl without a nose is at home.

But he doesn't mention that. His dad might start asking awkward questions about why his son is going to visit somebody who nobody but the ladies in the Pentecostal church mixes with.

Certain questions have to be avoided. If you don't want to tell lies, there's only one possible answer.

'I'll see,' says Joel. 'I haven't made up my mind yet, but I won't be long.'

That's a good answer. It's so vague that it can mean anything at all.

When he runs over the bridge he can't help but stop and gaze up at the arches soaring up above his head. A pity he hadn't scratched his name into the iron at the very top. If anybody else climbed up they would discover that they weren't the first to conquer the bridge.

When Joel gets to No-Nose's house, he notices that she's been trying to scrape the varnish off her currant bushes. And she's used shears to cut off the branches that had been completely choked by the varnish.

He pauses at the gate and tries to make up his mind what to say. He can't very well say they tipped the ants through her window because it was funny. That's a bad answer. An answer fit to make anybody angry.

Create fear, was what Ture had said. But he doesn't want to use Ture's words. He's not even sure he really understands what Ture meant. There's only one answer he can give. It's an answer that's both good and bad.

He can say that he doesn't know why he did it.

And even if he wasn't there when Ture smeared the currant bushes with varnish, he's not going to say so.

Ture doesn't exist.

He knocks on the door.

After a while, he knocks again.

Still nobody answers. There are lights in several windows, so she must be at home. Why doesn't she answer the door? He knocks one more time, belting the door quite hard now. Then he hears the gate squeaking.

He thinks it's Ture who's been

following him, but when he turns to look he sees that it's No-Nose. She has a big parcel under one arm.

'You've come at just the right time,' she says. 'Hold this parcel while I open the door. Make sure you don't drop it.'

She produces a large bunch of keys and picks one out. Joel thinks there must be at least fifty keys on the ring. She unlocks the door, and when they get into the hall he hands back the parcel.

'Joel,' she says. 'I thought you would come.'

Joel doesn't like it when other people know in advance what he's going to do. It's as if they can read his thoughts. They invade his most secret hiding place. His head.

'I just happened to be passing,' he says, and regrets it before he's even finished saying it. Nobody just happens to be passing in a cul-de-sac.

He decides to come straight to the point, and give her his explanation.

'I don't know why I did it,' he mumbles.

He'd really meant to say it in a loud,

firm voice, but something gives way in his throat. His voice breaks.

'That's all right,' she says. 'I know you won't do it again. Let's not speak any more about it. Take your shoes off and I'll show you what I've got inside this parcel.

She sneezes.

She puts her hand over her face and sneezes twice, three times.

How can you sneeze when you don't have a nose? Joel wonders. Does she sneeze through her mouth?

He follows her into the kitchen, which smells of heat. She carefully unwraps the parcel. It contains a globe.

'I found this in the attic at church,' she says. 'Nobody knows how it got there. Just look at this, though.'

She points at something on the surface of the globe. Somewhere in Africa, Joel sees. Somebody has made a little hole in Africa.

'I think that whoever made that hole used to live there,' she says. 'Maybe a missionary, a long, long time ago.'

Joel runs a finger over the globe, tracing seas and sounds and coasts.

'Samuel has been to all these places,' he says. 'I'm going there as well when I grow up. Samuel is my dad.'

'Do you know what it smells like there?' she asks.

She stands on a chair and unhooks a little leather pouch hanging over the cooker. She holds it under his nose, and he can smell the pungent aroma.

'Caraway seeds,' she says. 'They come from Zanzibar.'

She points at the globe, an island off the east coast of Africa.

Something suddenly occurs to him. How can she know what it smells like? She hasn't got a nose.

Once again she reads his thoughts.

'I can't smell anything any longer,' she says. 'But I can remember the smell of caraway seeds from when I was a child. Every time I see that pouch I remember the smell. You can smell things even if you don't have a nose.'

She lifts up the globe.

They both hear at the same time that there's something inside it.

A gold coin, Joel thinks. Or a pearl.

Or a lion's tooth . . .

The globe can be unscrewed into two halves.

'What do you think it is?' asks Gertrud.

Joel shakes his head. He doesn't know. But he hopes it's something exciting.

When Gertrude divides the two halves they find something that looks like a grain of sand. She picks it up and examines it under the kitchen light.

'A seed,' says Gertrud.

Joel is disappointed, but he doesn't show it. Gertrud laughs, as if she'd discovered the loveliest of pearls.

'It might be a seed from an orange tree,' she says. 'Or a tiny little flower . . .'

On the kitchen window ledge, the window through which they'd tipped in the ants, she has a flower pot. She pushes the seed gingerly into the soil.

'Perhaps it's still alive,' she says. 'Perhaps it will grow up and become a ginormous tree that eventually grows through the roof and spreads out its crown way above all the wooded hillsides . . .'

Joel starts telling her about his dad and all his travels. He tells the story of the water lilies on Mauritius, and the never-ending Congo River.

He wishes he could tell the stories as well as his dad can, but he can't find all the words he needs. Even so, he can see that she's listening intently, as if it had been Joel himself who'd experienced all the things he was talking about. Last of all he tells her about *Celestine*.

'You must show her to me one of these days,' she says.

Joel is surprised. How come that she seems to have forgotten all about the ants that he and Ture had tipped in through her kitchen window? Or the varnish that had ruined so many of her currant bushes? How was this possible?

And then he thinks that maybe he understands after all.

She's lonely. Everybody she meets in the street looks the other way. All she has is the women who go to the Pentecostal church.

How many people have ever sat in her kitchen in the evening and talked to her about seas and rivers that are far, far away?

It's hard to look at her face. The handkerchief she's stuffed into the hole where her nose ought to be is like a magnet. An eye magnet.

Even though he tries to look at her eyes or her forehead, all he seems to be able to see is the white handkerchief.

'It's OK, you can look,' she says. Then she stands up and goes to another room.

When she comes back she's taken the handkerchief away and replaced it with a red clown's nose. She's holding a lighted cigar.

'The only living steam engine in the world,' she says, taking a drag from the cigar.

When she exhales the smoke pours out of her red nose with a hissing sound.

Joel is astonished. Then he bursts out laughing. He can't help it.

She pulls a face and looks so funny

that he has to laugh. It's the best kind of laughter there is. Laughter that simply has to burst out.

When he prepares to leave, she asks him if he'd like to come again.

He nods. He thinks she's like The Old Bricklayer. Different. Somebody who does the unexpected.

Now he knows two people like that, he thinks as he walks home. And now that Ture is no longer around, he'll let them become members of The Secret Society.

When he gets home he finds *Celestine* standing on the kitchen table.

The logbook, he thinks. Now his dad has discovered the logbook! But Samuel just smiles at him.

'I know what you're thinking,' he says. 'I lifted her down because I thought she needed a good dusting. Then I saw that there was a book underneath her. I gathered it must be yours. It's still there. I promise you that I haven't opened it. We all have our secrets. If you take your boots off and sit down, I'll tell you one of my secrets. You should only reveal secrets when you really want to.'

He stretches out on the kitchen bench.

Joel unlaces his boots and sits down on his chair.

'That night when I was woken up and you were stuck on top of the bridge arch,' he says, 'it set me thinking about what it was like when I was eleven years old. That's a long time ago, many, many years ago. It took me some time to remember, but the memories came back in the end. When I was eleven my father, your grandad, was already dead. I've told you about that, how he drowned in a severe storm when his fishing boat capsized and sank. When I had my eleventh birthday, in December, it was terrible weather. There was a gale blowing, nearly a hurricane. When everybody had gone to bed I got dressed and sneaked out. We lived by the sea. The wind was howling and I was nearly blown over as I clambered over the rocks in the darkness. I remember thinking there was something very special about that night. Something was quite certainly going to happen. I climbed out onto the rocks nearest the sea. I lay down in a crevice and waited for something special to happen. I hadn't the slightest idea what it would be. Nor whether it would come from the sea or from the land or from the stars. I remember shivering with cold. And the only thing that happened was that I got colder and colder. In the end I had to stand up and go home. I recall being very disappointed. But when I snuggled down into bed I realised that something very special had happened, in fact. The special thing was that I'd ventured out onto the rocks in a hurricane. I'd done something I would never forget. I'd been lying in a crevice with a hurricane blowing, waiting for something special to happen. That was a big secret. I remember it now. And I've never mentioned it to a soul.'

'Not even to my mum?' asks Joel.

'Not even to Jenny.'

It seems to Joel that he's never talked to his dad like this before. Something has happened.

Something great, something

important. Something that grows and burns inside him, and makes him so excited that his face turns bright red.

Something that he can't note down in his logbook. Something that has nothing to do with words.

He knows now that he can ask awkward questions about Jenny, his mum. Or about Sara.

He's also certain that he can tell his dad that he doesn't want any sisters with Sara as their mother. He knows that difficult questions might not be quite so difficult any more. That doesn't mean that all the answers he gets will be what he wants to hear. But even so, maybe none of the answers will necessarily be awful. Bad perhaps, but not the kind of answers that turn his stomach over.

Today is a day he'll never forget. A special day. His and his dad's day.

'What do you reckon?' his dad asks. 'Is spring really on the way?'

'We must move to somewhere where we don't have snow all the time,' says Joel.

'We'll do that,' says his dad. 'We'll

move to somewhere where the sea never ices over . . .'

Joel checks the thermometer fixed outside the window. Minus one. That means spring can't be too far away. Another month and the first cowslips will be adding a touch of yellow to a dirty ditch. Only one more month . . .

*   *   *

And spring duly arrives. At long last.

One day Joel sees his first cowslip beside a ditch where the meltwater is bubbling downstream. The days get longer, and the black waters of the river start slowly forcing their way up through the thick covering of ice. Cracks appear in the white lid, and the floes start working their way free. Before long all the snow will have disappeared from the streets. The yellow local council lorries will sweep up the remains of the sand and gravel, and one day the first copious rains of spring will arrive. It will rain non-stop for at least twenty-four hours, and afterwards, the only remnants will be the remains of the piles at crossroads, and up against the cemetery wall.

One day the kitchen is lit up by the glow from an electric cooker.

The old wood-burning stove has been dumped in the garden, and Joel almost feels sorry for it. It's now surplus to requirements. If nobody finds a use for it, it will disappear under a covering of grass, and slowly disappear into the ground.

One day in the middle of April they go to the cycle shop, and The Flying Horse is still there in the window.

Joel sees that his dad is put out when he discovers the price; but he doesn't say a word, just takes out his wallet and pays up. Joel cycles home as proud as Punch.

That night when he rode the bike into a snowdrift and was rescued by The Old Bricklayer seems a very long way in the past.

As the nights get lighter, all the memories of winter fade away. Sometimes, in his dreams, Joel returns to the arch over the bridge. But when he wakes up and sees the faint light of dawn seeping in under the blinds, he's in no doubt that he's lying in bed and not clinging on to the arch.

He sometimes bumps into Ture.

They say hello, but they don't have a lot to talk about.

On one occasion Ture asks Joel if he wants to come and play in his big attic room. Joel says he'll come, but never gets round to it.

Joel and his friends have started playing at the deserted old brickworks again. They split up into Goodies and Baddies, and chase each other through the underground tunnels and The World of the Rusty Machines.

One of these days, Joel thinks. One of these days I might go round to Ture's again.

He's not going to run away. He'll stay here. He'll start school come autumn. Then, maybe. But not now . . .

In a month. In two. In three years.

In three years' time they'll be on their way, Joel and his dad.

Away from the house by the river that will never take them to the sea. Somewhere out there, perhaps, is

Jenny, Joel's mum.

Samuel tells Joel how it was.

'Maybe she was too young,' he says. 'I'd like to think so. Maybe when she had you, when she had a child, she was still a child herself? And maybe now, when she's no longer a child, maybe she regrets having run away? But she doesn't dare to come back, can't face looking her abandoned son in the eye.

'It's up to you,' he says. 'If you want to meet her, you have a right to do so, of course. If things are as I suspect they are, you are the only one who can help her to overcome her guilty conscience.'

'What about you?' asks Joel.

'It's different for me,' says his dad. 'It was so long ago. And now I have Sara.'

Sara with the red hat!

It's easier now, when his dad doesn't keep disappearing. Not least when Joel goes to the bar and sells newspapers. She tells the drinkers they ought to buy, and they do as they're told. Joel soon finds that he's saved up fifty kronor. He's never had as much money as that before.

Sara is fat, her breasts are too big and she has eczema. But she's a good cook and knows when Joel doesn't want to be patted on the cheek.

He can't understand why his dad is in such a good mood whenever he meets Sara—but then, he's realised that grown-ups are hard to fathom. Only the grown-ups who think like children and act differently are understandable.

Like Simon Windstorm and No-Nose Gertrud. Simon is old and Gertrud's a grown-up.

He can understand them, and enjoys being with them.

One evening when his dad is with Sara, Gertrud comes to visit Joel and he shows her *Celestine*. They examine her closely, and Joel tells Gertrud which are the most dangerous passages in all the seven seas . . .

*   *   *

Before he knows where he is, term comes to an end. It comes so quickly that it hasn't really registered until he wakes up one morning and realises that he doesn't have to go to school again until the autumn.

Then he leaps out of bed, gets dressed at top speed and cycles away on The Flying Horse.

Summer is boundless . . .

And the dog.

The dog that's heading for a star.

He never sees it again.

He thinks it might have been running so fast that it's already reached its star.

But then he thinks that this is a childish thought. Not something a nearly twelve-year-old ought to be thinking. But still.

He picks out a star shining brightly the other side of The Plough.

That's where his dog is.

He can't be childish for much longer, he knows that. Then his dog will vanish.

But it's still OK for now. He can still stop his bike and look up at the sky. And be confident that the dog got to where it was heading.

He likes that thought. It's a thought he'll never be able to share with anybody else. It's a thought that makes

258

him who he is, and nobody else.

I'm me, he thinks. And I can still spare a moment for a dog heading for a star. And getting there.

Then he rides off.

There's so much he has to do this summer . . .